PAUL MAGRS

ONE
MRS DANBY

My Dear Sister Nellie,

You had every faith in me. You knew I would do it, didn't you? Secretly I thought I would back out of this trip at the last moment. Too daunting for one such as I! However, I did not let my nerves get the better of me. And suddenly there I was, all alone, aboard the *SS Utopia*, in the dock at Southampton. Ready to sail the oceans at last and see the world. I don't know how I had the courage to set off like that, but somehow I did.

If I'd known what was coming, would I still have done it? I had no idea how brave I was going to have to be.

When the steward manhandled my bags all the way to my First Class cabin, he was full of reassurances. Blandishments, I would call them. How the sea would be calm and as smooth as a newly-made bed; how no storms were expected during our seven-night journey. But then, I expect they are used to soothing the nerves of first-time passengers like myself. Only a year after the ghastly tragedy of the *Titanic* – God rest their souls – I suppose most travellers experience qualms as they set sail upon vessels such as the *SS Utopia*, no matter how luxurious.

Why did I ever think an Atlantic passage would be something I'd enjoy?

I was rather fretful, Nellie. I sat up in my nicely appointed room and I couldn't sleep at all during my first night at sea. I listened to the ship's groaning, and panicked at every slight movement. I couldn't help wondering whether this trip of mine was such a good idea after all.

Only a month before, I had finally decided to throw caution to the wind. As you yourself pointed out, I'd hardly been anywhere in the world. Now that I found myself without employment or ties, it seemed the opportune moment for a lady of even my advanced years to sally forth into the wider world. Your enthusiastic goading worked, my dear sister. And so I went off in search of the New World, all alone.

But at the outset I couldn't help wondering: what if I had bitten off more than I could chew?

YOU WILL BE GLAD TO KNOW THAT I VENTURED FORTH ON THE THIRD DAY OF sailing. What a thrill it was to be out on the deck once the wind had died down. How I marvelled at that blue expanse of sky and sea, with absolutely nothing to mar the view. I took a brisk walk all around the *SS Utopia* and suddenly started feeling very much more comfortable than I had at first.

I saw my friendly steward and he showed me where breakfast was being served. I nibbled on a crumpet and sipped some rather superior tea and felt quite content, sitting alone. Lovely silver, I must say. And the tablecloths were beautifully pressed.

Such luxury! Who would have thought I would be enjoying such riches? Only the generosity of my erstwhile employer could have brought me here.

That dear man. Though, as you have rightly pointed out, sister, I deserved every penny of my severance pay. My years as his housekeeper were not uneventful, and sometimes they were downright terrifying. One never knew who would be turning up to consult with him in his sitting room. Traipsing muck up and down my stair carpet. Murderers and poisoners and suchlike. I was in far more danger than I think I ever knew about. But bless him, anyhow, and I hope he's doing well tending his insects in Sussex. I had an extra spoonful of delicious honey on my last crumpet in honour of my ex-employer and his current charges.

Then I saw that I had attracted the attention of a gentleman at the next table. He, too, was eating alone, a clean-shaven, hawk-faced chap wearing evening dress for breakfast. He was peering at me over his pince-nez, so I shot him one of my basilisk stares – you know the ones, dear Nellie – and he disappeared once more behind his Times. Honestly! A Peeping Tom. And in First Class, too.

I wondered who he was. Quite a dapper gent.

THAT NIGHT I ATTENDED A CONCERT WEARING MY DRESSIEST GOWN AND, AS YOU promised, I soon fell into company. I was set upon by some women from the north country. Bradford, they informed me. The wives of some manufacturers of woollen garments. There was talk of mills and some such. I told them that I have a sister in North Yorkshire, on the very coast, and they made interested noises, all the way through the programme of light classics.

The small orchestra was tuneful and energetic, and I couldn't help but be reminded of the band that bravely played on as the *Titanic* went down to her ignominious end. A gloom crept over me. And it wasn't helped by those fussy Yorkshire women and their urgent quizzing, which began during a medley of waltzes. As you know, Strauss always makes me queasy, and that feeling wasn't helped by the realization that these blowsy types had learned from shipboard gossip of my name and previous occupation.

They were avid for details of what it must have been like, keeping house for "the Great Man himself", as they styled him. Well, I could have told them a tale or two about the messy and dirty circumstances in which that Great Man liked to languish, given half a chance. I could have told them about gunshots and smashed windows in the early watches of the night. But I thought – why bother? I don't need the friendship of this gaggle of nosey parkers. I am on this trip to find a new life. Not to dwell upon the vicissitudes of the old.

I slipped out during a break for refreshments and returned to my cabin. I got somewhat lost as I traipsed down those endless corridors, and that was when I came upon that man again. The one who had been staring as I broke my fast. Perhaps, I thought, he too knew of my connection to the Great Detective. It was galling, really, to have been nothing but an invisible helpmeet all my life and yet then, when I could have done with some peace, to be drawing unwanted attention like this.

I clapped eyes on him as he came creeping out of a door clearly marked 'crew only'. The pointy-nosed cove was still in the same jacket as he had worn that very morning, and he had a suspicious look about him. Evidently he had been poking about down in the bowels of the *Utopia*, up to no good. In one hand he was clutching a fearsomely pointed stick. This he quickly hid behind his back as I coughed loudly and swept past him in my formal gown: my magenta with the whalebone support and the seed pearl embroidery. You admired it, Nellie, remember?

He bade me good evening and I gave him another of my stares.

He was, I thought then, not a very nice gentleman. I have a keen sense of villainy, of course, due to my many years at Balcombe Street. As you know, I can tell at a glance what's lurking in the murkiness of a man's soul. You, my dear sister, could do with some of that perspicacity yourself.

Do look after yourself, in that seaside resort of yours. I am so far away and feel uncomfortable because I can't advise you if you start making a fool of yourself again. You were never very shrewd when it came to the male sex and their heinous desires.

I decided to take to my bed as the tossing sea turned rough and everything started to roll to the rhythm of awful Strauss.

THERE WE WERE IN THE MIDDLE OF THE ATLANTIC OCEAN. THERE WAS NOTHING to see, in whichever direction one looked. Never had I had so little to do, or had so few concerns. It was a strangely liberating feeling, marred only by the suspicion that the *Titanic* must have been hereabouts when disaster struck. Also, by the dread I felt for reaching our destination. Oh yes, indeed, I had dreamed about this holiday and experiencing the New World for a long time. But, really, what did I think would happen there? I was all alone, Nellie. With no one at all to share those new sights and experiences with. I found myself thinking about the years ahead – and wondering what I might fill them with. I am no longer needed, Nellie. I am redundant in every sense.

WELL, OBVIOUSLY I CAME TO MY SENSES AND SAW THAT IT WAS NO GOOD CARRYING on like that. Neither of us was brought up to wallow in feelings of desperation. And so it was that, determined to clear my head of all this foolish anguish, I took my daily constitutional, five times round the deck of our ship. I nodded and smiled to those passengers whose faces had become familiar in those past few days; I paused to examine the ship's daily manifest; and I watched some elderly gentlemen playing a doddering game of quoits. And then, as I reached the very prow of our vessel, I was interrupted in my reverie by that same pale-faced chap with the pointed nose. That day he was in a green velvet smoking jacket, and I had the instant impression that he had planned this interception.

He opened his mouth to explain himself, but I wasn't having any of it. I waved him off and tried to bustle past. I felt a bit foolish running away, but a woman alone can't take too many chances. There he was, rabbiting on about why he'd been carrying that sharpened stick and sneaking about, and I tried to tell him I just didn't care. But then he said it. He said it in such a sharp, commanding voice: 'Mrs Martha Danby. Please let me explain.'

I turned round to look at him, amazed that he knew who I was. He was glaring at me with these steely grey eyes. Then I thought, well, anyone can look at the ship's passenger list, can't they?

He stepped forward and I was holding my breath. The sun was bright on his slicked-back white hair. I did think him a tad attractive, Nellie, for an older gent. But I didn't want to let that show. He was burbling on about carrying pointed sticks and knives... Heavens! He opened up his jacket to show me that, stitched into the silk lining, he had a deadly array of hunting knives and more of those pointed sticks.

I boggled at him, Nellie. This was a very oddly-equipped gentleman. He was telling me that I had nothing to fear. His job was to protect ladies like myself. This was why he was armed so fearsomely. It was his role in this world to combat evil and the forces of darkness, wherever he was. Even aboard a luxury sailing vessel like this one.

Forces of darkness, I thought. Here we go again. Well, Nellie, I swiftly made my excuses and hastened to leave. I don't know why he'd decided I needed to see his arsenal out there on the prow, but I wasn't going to hang around.

'Wait!' he cried out. And then he asked me, urgently, whether I wasn't in fact the very same Mrs Martha Danby who had worked for so many years as housekeeper to the esteemed Mr Nightshade Jones of 221b Balcombe Street.

Graciously, I gave the nod. 'And Mr Wilson, too,' I added. Folk tend to leave out the good doctor, but I was at his beck and call, as well. And this polite gentleman with the stakes and knives nodded thoughtfully. He'd come over all funny at the mere thought of Mr Jones. I wondered if he was an acquaintance or something... or worse... an enemy! A deadly enemy who had waited in the shadows until he could get this helpless female housekeeper alone...

He told me had conceived the greatest respect for my employers and myself. And then he introduced himself, rather charmingly, I thought. His name is Doctor Abraham Van Halfling. A Doctor, I thought, Nellie! A doctor of medicine and he's got a PhD in ancient folklore and a Chair in Metaphysics to boot. Not that I know what a Chair in Metaphysics is, but it sounds rather grand.

I allowed him to take me in to lunch and we had a fine time of it, Nellie. He ate very little himself, but ordered all sorts of delicacies that he thought I ought to try. What a cultivated chap! Calling out for things in French without a qualm. Things that I didn't even recognize. It was like Manna from Heaven, Nellie. It was like ambrosia or something. And all the while this dapper gentleman told me all about his scientific investigations. Not that I followed a word. Terribly well-groomed, he was.

He walked me back to my cabin and the sea was a little wilder, so I had a rolling gait as we made our way through the narrow corridors. Nothing to do with the crisp German wines he'd insisted I sample. However, I did feel slightly tipsy and perhaps over-stimulated by the company and the attention I'd received. I was much in need of my afternoon nap as we rounded the last corner before my door. I was fiddling in my clutch bag for my key just as that friendly steward I mentioned to you came walking past us.

The ship lurched, and I clutched the brass rail and dropped my key. At that very moment I saw that Doctor Van Halfling – my gallant companion – had produced, from inside his velvet jacket one of his sharpened sticks. I gave a shriek. I thought he was about to impale me, Nellie.

But he swung himself round and plunged that weapon straight into my steward. The stake went into the clean white breast of his jacket. Right into his heart. The sailor looked amazed and he gave a horrible, gurgling scream. And then POOF. He exploded into a shower of grey particles, which dropped to the carpet outside my cabin door.

Abraham Van Halfling was still holding his stake. He looked grimly satisfied. 'These evil creatures are everywhere, Mrs Danby. And that is why I am always quiveringly alert.

'What evil creatures?' I asked him.

'Why, vampires, Mrs Danby,' said he.

TWO
VAN HALFLING

From the journal of doctor abraham van halfling

T<small>ODAY HAS BEEN A GOOD DAY ABOARD THE</small> *SS Utopia*. O<small>UR JOURNEY ACROSS THE</small>
Atlantic had been fairly uneventful until this morning. Then, as I suspected they
would, my enemies declared their vile, stinking hand.

Tonight, one fewer member of the undead walks the Earth. I dispatched him
with all due haste, once I knew who he was. I had kept my eyes open for days.
Looking for the classic signs. Dogging his very steps. Waiting for the optimum
moment when I could plunge a trusty stake into his chest and reduce him to dust.

It was one of the stewards, in First Class. Ach, the ancient curse of vampirism
is no respecter of social standing. Anyone can fall prey to its taint. So it was with
this luckless steward who – I am glad to report – will trouble the living no more.
He was not, however, alone on this luxurious vessel, I know. We are carrying
others of his ilk into the New World, where they will spread their filthy practices

and appetites, as they have done for untold generations in the old.

But today has been a good day. One of the better days. A day when I could prove that, even in my advanced state of decrepitude, Abraham Van Halfling can still stare the dreaded beast in the eye and poke a pointed stick at it.

Yet I grow old and befuddled. I am tired, as if battling that creature has drained away some of my own precious life force. My dear granddaughter asked me, before I left her on the dock at Southampton, whether I would be strong enough for this journey. It is a question I have asked myself. Do I still have the energy to endure this lecture tour I have promised to undertake? Visiting thirty-three states of the Union in two months. It seems rather a lot, all of a sudden. And the public speaking engagements are the least of it. For I know that, wherever I go, the undead will not be far away. Already they know that I am on my way to the United States and they will be anticipating my arrival with savage glee...

I sit at my desk tonight, looking out of the portal at the wine dark sea and the moonlight over the Atlantic. A chilling, lonely sight. Perhaps I should have stayed in England with my granddaughter, Jessica. Perhaps I should hide myself away from the creatures of the night and pray they do not come looking for me. Ach, tonight I feel terribly alone...

Except that on the SS Utopia I have made the acquaintance of a most charming lady. I noticed her on the day of our departure, looking very self-assured and immaculately groomed. She was going up the gangplank, just ahead of me. I noticed her at several meals and a recital the other evening. Imagine my pleasure and surprise then, when I discovered this lady's identity. She is Mrs Martha Danby, erstwhile housekeeper to the renowned Balcombe Street detective, Mr Nightshade Jones.

Imagine being in the presence of such a genius on a daily basis! And being around him as he worked on his most famous cases. He is the only criminal investigator in the world whom I admire. I find detectives in the main a prosaic and pettifogging species. But Jones knows more than any of them. And I had hoped that, one day, perhaps, I would have the honour of meeting him and even working with him. Perhaps there would be a case with a supernatural taint or a satanic bent... and the great logician would be forced to take advice from one such as I. One steeped in the lore and arcana of the invisible world...

But, alas, Jones is retired and living in Sussex, by all reports. His great mind tinkers no more with insoluble problems. But here is his housekeeper, set loose upon the world. Meeting her is, to me, almost second best. And besides, she is a charming and rather attractive lady of advanced years. I would say she was about my age. What a delectable companion she would make for the rest of this voyage.

However, I think, perhaps, I might have gone about the business of getting to know her in a rather unfortunate manner. I was keen to demonstrate that, even in the midst of perfidious danger, I was able and prepared to defend her to the death. I showed her the array of vampire-slaying paraphernalia I always carry about my person. The poor dear looked rather alarmed and I realized with a sick dread that she imagined that I was some kind of crazed maniac. Most unfortunate.

I needed to convince her that the deadly danger was all around her and that I was not the source of it. Wherever Van Halfling goes, he is dogged and tormented by those undead souls who wish to revenge their noxious selves upon him. And so it was that Mrs Martha Danby was present when I was forced to whip out a stake and kill the First Class Steward in the corridor outside her cabin. This was just after lunch and she admitted, rather biliously, that her Sole Veronique was rising in her gorge. Freddie, she said the steward had been called, and he had been quite the favourite with her.

I helped her into her cabin and she was understandably wary of me. I tried to explain that the sailor had been a monster. A vicious killer. One with his sights undoubtedly set upon her. She touched her neck self-consciously and asked, 'Are there really such things as vampires, then?'

I nodded grimly. She had seen for herself, surely. No natural, living animal goes POOF like that and turns into dust when staked through the heart. What more evidence did she need? Would she have to see the fangs? Feel them tearing out her throat?

The poor old lady sat down on her tidily-made bed. I felt uncomfortably aware that I was intruding upon a lady's boudoir. Embarrassed, I brushed some flaky crumbs of ash from my smoking jacket.

Mrs Danby had a flask of medicinal brandy in her handbag and this I helped her with, noting how her hands trembled. I thought about calling for some tea to be brought to us, but decided that this might draw attention to the loss of one of the ship's complement of serving staff.

I tried to explain to Mrs Danby, and she listened. I told her that my life has been spent in the sometimes hopeless-seeming task of ridding the world of this undead filth. For decades I have fought with monsters, demons and vampires, all over the world. I have, in my own small way, become renowned for my dangerous encounters. Nowhere near as famed as Mrs Danby's previous employer, but I am not unknown for my vampire-slaying endeavours.

I was gratified that Mrs Danby knew a little of my work. She seemed to recall that that Great Detective himself had kept a manila folder of documents and cuttings relating to some of my cases. I was utterly delighted by this, and tried to hide my excitement at the very thought. 'Mr Jones didn't hold with messing about in the supernatural, though,' she added, darkly, draining her tooth glass of brandy. 'But he knew it was out there. And he knew that you were combating it.' She nodded at me thoughtfully, and added, 'I thought I recalled your name from somewhere.'

Then she was overcome by tiredness. As well she might be, after a shock like she had undergone, and a big lunch too, followed by brandy. I left her to her slumbers and patrolled the ship for the rest of the day. My ear was cocked, avid for gossip about the missing steward and alert for loose talk about any other undead aboard. Because there will indeed be others on this ship, mark my words. Ach, they will not rest easy now that one of them is slain.

I WAS SURPRISED, THAT EVENING, TO RECEIVE A MESSAGE FROM MRS DANBY. I HAD just finished writing the above journal entry, when another steward – a perfectly harmless one this time, thank goodness – rapped on my cabin door. Mrs Danby's note asked me to take supper with her in the Polynesian Dining Room on Deck B. Not an eatery I was familiar with. I hurriedly made myself respectable and went to meet her there, amongst the fake palm trees and the wickerwork furniture.

Mrs Martha Danby looked resplendent in cerise taffeta. When I bowed stiffly she invited me to sit on one of the rather low chairs and waved to the waiter. We were to drink some exotic cocktails and have a bite to eat together. She wanted to thank me, she said. At lunchtime she had been much too alarmed to do so, and had been rather rude. I had saved her life from that abominable monster in the corridor, clearly, and I deserved some kind of reward.

I demurred, naturally, telling her that this was my duty upon the Earth. I am pledged to combat these dark forces wherever I go. Even though I would rather quietly retire, the revenants from hell will not let me go.

Mrs Danby shook her head and sighed, and sipped her bright green cocktail through a straw.

Together we had a rather pleasurable evening, soon managing to veer away from the unsavoury topic of the undead. I was keen to hear something of Mrs Danby's experiences of working for the Great Detective and, to my surprise, she grew loquacious on the subject. She had two high spots of red on her cheeks – either from excitement at relating these old adventures, or from the heady drinks we were taking. Either way, the effect was most becoming.

I can hardly remember what we ate. Some kind of sticky chops, I think. Messy and picky food, but all of my attention was on my beguiling companion. A mere housekeeper of course, but a repository for all kinds of amazing tales and secrets.

After our supper we decided to take a turn or two round the deck, where others were strolling peacefully under the gentle radiance of the full moon. It was a perfectly still night. There was hardly even a whisper of a breeze. Mrs Danby and I linked arms and she told me how safe she felt in my presence. Even though she knew there were monsters aboard, waiting to jump out and slake their unnatural thirsts, with my arm linked through hers, she felt quite safe and calm.

And so we walked about the deck and all the while, I was foolishly composing in my head the next postcard I would send to my granddaughter, Jessica. I would tell her that – just as she had predicted – I had seemingly embarked upon what might be called a shipboard romance. When Jessica had playfully suggested such a thing I had laughed it off, feeling rather cross, if truth be told. It is a long time since the very idea of romance flickered through the mind of Abraham Van Halfling. My life is too fraught and beset by danger. Ach, I could never expose a loved one to the deadly horrors I face each day.

And yet I was enjoying the sensation of walking alongside this talkative housekeeper. I liked the pressure of her arm linked through mine. The sound of her sensible shoes clopping on the wooden deck. Here I was, possessor of arguably the finest mind in Europe when it comes to matters of the unseen and the arcane... secretly thrilled as I took a stroll with a woman who was, in the end, a mere domestic servant.

I broached, once again, the subject of Messrs Jones and Wilson, longing to know more about the marvellous things Mrs Danby must have heard.

She chuckled indulgently and patted my arm. 'Oh, mostly I heard a lot of shouting and name-calling, nothing very sensible. They were like two over-grown schoolboys.' She looked up at me earnestly and added, 'You must call me Martha, you know.'

I nodded at her and smiled, feeling rather self-conscious. 'Martha,' I repeated.

And just then, at that very intimate moment, a terrible shudder ran through the deck. The whole of the *SS Utopia* gave what felt like a profound shiver, and there was a screeching noise that lasted no less than ten seconds. It was the most horrible, penetrating noise I have ever heard, and I didn't dare imagine what it portended.

Cries of alarm went up all over the top deck. I heard a scream and a shout. Passengers were milling, and starting to panic. A warning klaxon went off briefly, and then was stilled. Before me, Martha's face turned a deadly shade of white. Then the alarm bells started ringing with great purpose. There came louder cries and shrieks. We ran to the side and looked about desperately. But there was nothing to be seen.

Martha said the precise thing I was thinking just then: 'We've struck something. Just like the *Titanic* did! Oh my goodness!'

And I knew in my soul that she was right.

THREE
PROFESSOR
ZARATHUSTRA

To my Darling Wife, Mrs George Edward Zarathustra,

Confound them and blast them all to hell!

Why can't they just leave me alone? Why is it that every expedition of mine is ruined by clumsy fools? Why is every little scheme thwarted and spoiled by dunderheads and ninnies?

All I want is peace and quiet, and a chance to test out my theories and ideas. I do not ask for much. Just that everyone keeps out of my way! Just that I – the greatest genius of my age – be allowed to continue with my thoughts and experiments away from the common herd, undisturbed by them. Is that too much to ask?

Even here! Even out here, in the middle of the vastness of the Atlantic Ocean, they will not leave me alone. My darling, you will not believe what has happened this evening. It beggars all belief and yet merely confirms me in my attitude of utter scorn for the hopelessness of the common ruck of mankind!

Forgive me, my dear, for yet another ranting letter from your doting husband. You with your meekness, patience and kindness. I imagine you sitting at our breakfast table, at home in London, reading my latest missive.

Now, my dear, these letters to you are to be my official record of my current adventures. You will be the recipient of my firsthand reports about all that becomes of me. I may at times seem to be telling you things about myself and my preparations for this mission that you already know but I believe that with your infinite and gentle patience you will not grow vexed with me. For I am addressing not only you, Mrs Zarathustra, but posterity herself with these pages!

Over the many years of our blissful union I have sent you similar letters from all over the world. From my expeditions to the North and South Poles, from the most arid deserts and the loftiest peaks, and from the heart of the Lost World of antediluvian animals itself.

From all of these places I have sent you word of my doings, and you have read them knowing that they came with my love – even when I was ranting against the idiocy of my companions or the temerity of my enemies.

This, however, has to be the worst obstacle I have encountered yet.

They have bumped into my submersible.

MY SUBMERSIBLE!

I worked for years on this vessel. Designing and taking great pains with its every aspect. I brought in the finest craftsmen and supervised every stage of the work myself. I spent almost all of our remaining funds on this unique and futuristic vehicle. I re-mortgaged our townhouse in Greenwich, where you now sit, taking your morning coffee and reading of my vexed adventures.

Everything we have has been poured into this submersible. It is the most wonderful craft ever devised for travelling through the world's endless oceans. It is small, only the size of a baker's van, I would say, but it is equipped with all the most sophisticated scientific equipment I could afford. All for exploring the profound depths of the oceans that span our globe. But, my dear, I hardly need repeat all of these details to you, who never once complained, since you understood as only the most loyal wife on Earth could understand, the vital importance of my work. You also understand that only George Edward Zarathustra is up to the task of probing the unknown immensities of water and discovering the strange life forms hidden within! Only he is brave and clever enough! And so I set forth, from the Thames Estuary last New Year's Day, and bade you a fond farewell, my dear.

Now I am halfway across the Atlantic. I am quite near my intended site of investigation. The very place I set out to explore. But then – just as I prepared to dive down, down, down to the very depths...

They crashed into me.

AAAAaaagggghhhhhh!!!

Who were they? Well, let me tell you.

They were the *SS Utopia*. The most luxurious ocean-going vessel still afloat. Though they came quite close, this evening, to being afloat no longer. Tonight their captain, Timperley, was very nearly responsible for a tragedy at sea, so soon after the sinking of the *Titanic*. The fool paid no heed to my submersible and struck me as I tried furiously to veer out of his way.

Such a tiny craft, after all, compared with the hugeness of the *Utopia*. I could have been punctured and split and cast aside in the wake of the gigantic liner. But a miracle must have occurred because, though my ship scraped along the hull of the liner and there was a hideous noise, no one died. This is some consolation, I suppose.

But I fear the submersible is damaged beyond all repair. It was sent spinning round and round through the churning waters and I – almost senseless from the collision – had to wrestle manfully with her poor, disoriented controls.

When the chips are down, George Edward Zarathustra always rises to the occasion, as you well know. I managed to pilot my poor submersible up to the surface. We broke into the open air with a great splash and the moonlight was blinding to me. I have become used to the twilight of deep regions, and this sudden emergence into the open air came as quite a shock.

I grappled with the mechanisms of the hatchway and flung it open. Then I found that my brass sphere was bobbing along gently, not too far from the giant ocean cruiser. I blinked in the starlight and gazed up at the ship. Passengers in evening dress were out on the decks, and they were waving energetically at me. A few were starting to applaud and call out 'Bravo, sir!' My sudden appearance in the water was some cause for celebration. It grew louder and more sustained and all at once it was clear that every single one of the passengers and crew aboard that ship recognized me and was aware of my fame!

However, not even such a rapturous greeting could put me at my ease just yet. The damage to my private property was yet to be assessed and I wasn't quite mollified. My submersible houses such a plenitude of incredibly intricate instruments and gauges. Her workings are infinitely sensitive, and seemed to have been knocked out of all kilter by the force of the glancing blow she had taken. I dreaded to look at them. All I could bring myself to do was make sure that we were not taking on water. We weren't. But several display screens and control panels had been shattered and ruined. I vowed that someone was going to be made to pay for them.

I hoisted myself more fully out of the hatchway and bellowed up at the decks of the *Utopia*: 'Take me to your captain! I am Professor George Edward Zarathustra and I have a serious complaint to lodge against him!'

I was pleased to hear further gasps of recognition, even excitement and delight, when I shouted my name across the choppy expanse of water between the ship and my sub. Certain spectators were only just catching up with the fact that there was a celebrated scientist-adventurer in their midst. I doubt that there was a single soul on board unaware of the name and the exploits of yours truly. I risk life and limb regularly in the pursuit of knowledge, danger and enlightenment! I certainly deserved the cascades of applause that I received when the sailors threw ropes out to my poor submersible and tethered her to their side.

I thoroughly deserved their plaudits as I climbed up the rope ladder they threw down for me. I felt rather dizzy and sick, my dear, as you well might imagine, after spending days underwater and then being knocked about like that. Oh, but how they roared their approval at old Zarathustra as he clambered manfully up those ropes and then stood, at last, without a drop of seawater on him, upon the deck of the SS *Utopia*! Hurrah!

I MUST ADMIT, I WAS PLEASED TO STRETCH MY LIMBS ON THIS MUCH LARGER vessel. For weeks now I have been feeling rather cramped aboard my submersible. It felt good to have a steaming hot bath and share in some of the luxuries with which the *Utopia* is stuffed.

Above decks, I knew they were manhandling my craft aboard and setting it down carefully, as per my instructions. I had commandeered the tennis courts for the purpose and made my demands quite clear. They were to give me all the help they could to make my submersible seaworthy again. I took Captain Timperley aside and berated him in the strongest terms. It turned out that he quite understood my point. Indeed, I think he would have been happy with anything I suggested. He looked extremely pleased to have someone as infamous as me aboard his ship. I would go so far as to say that he looked agitated, even nervous, in my presence. He quite properly asked me to sit at the captain's table for dinner the following evening. I think him rather a fool, to be honest, but at least he is doing as I dictate.

My dear, this ship is teeming with lazy, decadent people. They loll about all day long as if they hadn't a care in the world. They eat the finest foods and drink the finest wines known to mankind, and they think of nothing but pleasuring themselves all the way to New York. Now, I am as fond of the finer things in life as the next man, but these people turn my stomach. They are much too pampered and spoiled.

Except... The next morning when I had emerged from a restful night's sleep and had changed into a clean shirt and suit, I ventured up onto deck and ran across two people that I wouldn't class in the same category as the rest of the passengers. Not at all. They are two rather remarkable individuals, truth be told, and I was pleased to bump into them.

I soon discovered that it was they who sought me out, having been part of the crowd the previous night, watching agog from the ship as my submersible bobbed along beside the *Utopia*. They had recognized me – and were both keen to speak with me. Mrs Martha Danby I already knew slightly, of course. In years past I have given her my hat and cloak to look after as I have stepped into the hallowed downstairs hall of Nightshade Jones' dwelling place. Several times she has brought me a cup of tea and a biscuit to nibble on – on her very best china – as I have sat in consultation with that famed detective. She has probably been witness to several of the violently loud arguments I have enjoyed with her employer. Now here she is on the *SS Utopia*, looking rather pink and healthy, and clearly glad to be away from smoky, dirty, dangerous London.

She even gave me a brief peck on the cheek when we were reunited. I suspect that the old lady has harboured a keen attraction for me for several years, and only now did she feel bold enough to express it. Well, you needn't feel envious, my poor dear wife! She is a shrewish and shrivelled creature, though friendly enough! Why, no wonder she just about keeled over and almost fainted at the sight of George Edward Zarathustra! I looked my very manliest best this morning in my brilliant white safari suit.

Mrs Danby and her companion were lavish in their praise of my submersible, which I allowed them to examine at closer quarters. I took them to the tennis courts, where a light steam was lifting off its rivets and joints as it sat there in the morning sun and my heart longed to be aboard her again – away from all this pansyish luxury – and thrusting down, down, down into the Stygian underwater gloom.

'I don't think I'd like to be cooped up aboard that,' chuckled Mrs Danby's companion. He was a whey-faced, skinny old wretch with a bony face and a pointed nose. When I glared at him I suddenly realized who he was. I broke out in a delighted grin and slapped him on the back, which set him off on a coughing fit and almost knocked him over.

'You are the vampire hunter! Van Halfling!' I roared with pleasure. I had heard tell of his grislier exploits several times from fellow adventurers. I had even longed to explore his nocturnal world of nightmare creatures for myself one day. It was on my list of things to do.

Van Halfling didn't say much, but I could tell the old fella was cheered by my knowing who he was. Mrs Danby interrupted and asked what it was I was engaged in. Knowing me, she said, I was on the trail of something absolutely amazing. She was desperate to hear about it.

I beamed at her. In fact, I beamed at them both. And I thought – well, what harm is there in coming clean? I instinctively trusted these two people. I shall tell them straight out what it is I am looking for. I shall disclose the very reason that I'm trawling the Atlantic in a craft no bigger than a baker's van.

'I,' I told them, 'am hunting for the magnificent and ancient city that I know lies directly beneath these waves! Fathoms beneath the surface, there is a fabulous world quite alien to us all and never suspected by mankind. What do you think of that then, eh?'

Van Halfling and Mrs Danby simply stared at me. Though they didn't say anything, I could tell that they were both tremendously impressed. And they knew, too, that if it came from the mouth of George Edward Zarathustra, then it had to be true! They were delighted that I had revealed my secret to them! And in that instant I just knew that the three of us were fated to be fellow adventurers!

How right I was! What followed next was to be one of my most diabolical adventures ever!

FOUR
MRS DANBY

My Dear Sister Nellie,

My dear, it is time this long letter of mine told you more about my ill-fated Atlantic My dear, it is time this long letter of mine told you more about my ill-fated Atlantic Crossing. I am so glad that there is no such thing as instantaneous transmission of letters across the ocean. Imagine if I had been able to send word of my terrifying adventures to you in dribs and drabs! You'd have been so worried to hear what was happening to me if my accounts came in shorter instalments.

That night aboard the *SS Utopia* I had dinner with that dapper older gentleman with whom I have become acquainted. It was a charming evening, and he was quite the flatterer. Afterwards we took a turn around the deck in the moonlight. But, Nellie, it wasn't the evening's potentially romantic entanglements that were of the greatest import, but a near-fatal collision that the *SS Utopia* had with a home-made submersible, which was – at that very moment – bobbing to the surface!

Luckily, both Captain Timperley and the owner of the mysterious submarine managed to avert disaster. The small underwater craft and its owner were hauled aboard – and all we onlookers applauded with relief as a rather bulky gentleman dragged himself up on deck. Nellie – it was a celebrity. The famed Professor Zarathustra, no less! I knew him at once, with his immensely impressive physique and his gigantic facial hair. Well, you would know him too, Nellie. Haven't you pored over the pictures and stories in the more sensational papers, detailing his exploits and adventures? And I have been in his presence before, though only in a very humble capacity, when he has descended upon Mr Jones's quarters in order to consult my employer during an adventure or two. I don't think he would have ever noticed me, Nellie, on those few occasions. And now here he is – the bravest and cleverest man in all the Empire. Aboard this very ship. We are in the presence of greatness. Quite a few folk were laughing at his dishevelled appearance as he bobbed along in his little submarine beside us. They pointed and jeered at him, and I worried that the adventurer's feelings might be hurt by all of this unlooked-for attention.

Waking up the following morning, taking breakfast with the other First Class passengers, I was intrigued to discern a palpable sense of excitement on board. The rather more select travellers were aware that we had a famed hero in our midst and – this was the most spectacular turn of events, as I thought at the time – I myself was being introduced to him, Nellie! Upon that very morning. I could barely credit it, and I don't suppose you can either, as you read this. Your own humble sister. Not as a servant or a housekeeper, but as an equal. I have shaken the hand of the eminent and well-nigh legendary Zarathustra.

At the time, I was astonished by my good fortune.

I was up on deck with that elderly Van Halfling again. Charming he may be, but I do find his conversation somewhat repetitive at times. What is more, he will insist on discussing the most morbid and horrid subjects, even when the sun is shining brilliantly and I am wearing my nicest sundress and hat, which he hasn't seen fit to comment on once. It was an outfit I was saving for the sunniest day aboard the ship, which today has proved to be.

Luckily, I was looking quite my best when we happened to bump into Professor Zarathustra. He looked rather splendid himself, in an eau de nil linen suit and an intensely glowering expression.

This is the moment that sent my senses reeling, Nellie. He recognized me! He stared into my eyes as he took my hand and I believe he recognized me at once. Not as a mere domestic servant, but as a woman in her own right! I felt quite giddy, I can tell you.

Van Halfling looked rather pinched and sour-faced during this encounter, even though Zarathustra turned to him and congratulated him on his long career of hunting phantoms. He needn't have looked so left out!

Then Professor Zarathustra started saying the most astonishing things about the investigation he was in the midst of undertaking, and he led us to his marvellous little submarine, expounding at length about his mission. Well, as I already knew from the papers and from Mr Jones's occasional pronouncements on the subject, Professor Zarathustra gets up to some improbable things. But that morning, Nellie, he was telling us his wild theories to do with a gigantic city deep down beneath the waves! Van Halfling looked thoughtful and, at times, sceptical, but I was – I admit – carried away by the romance of it all. A sunken city, Nellie! A lost world deep down below our feet!

We took elevenses together and the Professor was good enough to ask me about my journey and my plans, and he also quizzed Van Halfling about his affairs. Then suddenly he was on his feet, declaring that he must set to work on his underwater vehicle at once. The instrumentation aboard had been knocked out of alignment by the rough handling he had received last night and so the Professor must presently bring his expertise to bear upon mechanical matters.

Before he left he clapped Van Halfling heartily on the back (leaving the old cove rather shaken!) and then he gently took my hand (tiny in his huge, hairy paw) and kissed it. Oh, to feel his black beard bristling on the back of my hand, Nellie. You'll think I went schoolgirlish and soft, but there was something about that man's very presence that could turn me that way. Perhaps it was the impressive bulk of him, or his charisma, or the awareness of his prodigious brain, ticking away inside that great skull. Whatever it was, to be in his actual, physical presence seemed to me like a rare treat.

I was, of course, to revise that opinion fairly soon afterwards.

But at the time I was like a mimsy fool.

When he stomped away – intent on fixing his submersible – I was left alone with Van Halfling. I believed the old man was in a sulk. I announced that I would be taking a nap this afternoon, and I left him there and then, alone with the empty cups and saucers.

But I didn't nap. I flew back to my writing desk to try to note down my feelings about the encounter, intending to continue my letter to you. But I couldn't concentrate or get it all satisfactorily down on paper. I couldn't doze, either, because I was all of a dither. The excitement was considerable. And there was even more to come, Nellie. For, just then, as I was scrawling away, a thick, creamy envelope was pushed under my cabin door. Beautiful copperplate handwriting on the invitation within.

I had been summoned to the Captain's Table for dinner that very evening!

Was it any wonder that I couldn't nap? Oh, I thought, isn't this just the life? And it was true, Nellie, at that moment everything seemed absolutely marvellous.

I AM WRITING THIS SOME WHILE AFTER THE EVENTS OF THAT NIGHT. THEY ARE still extremely vivid to me. Just by closing my eyes I can picture everything that went on. I can hear the screams. I can feel the icy cold shock of what we fully supposed to be our final doom.

I don't believe I am exaggerating when I tell you that on that very night, things aboard the SS *Utopia* took a rather untoward turn.

We were in the main dining room, between our main course and our pudding. There was I, in my finest frock, hugely pleased and honoured to be seated at the Captain's table. Various dignitaries and millionaires were seated at the same table, and I was trying my utmost not to feel intimidated or out of my depth. Here was the now-familiar form of Doctor Van Halfling, and there was an empty space for Professor Zarathustra, who had also been invited to dine with Captain Timperley and who was apparently late.

Captain Timperley was a most engaging fellow. Seated to my right, he inclined his head towards me as I answered his polite enquiries about my humble and rather humdrum life. He was such a gentleman that he carried on as if I were the most fascinating woman in the world.

All was fine, until the brusque arrival of Professor Zarathustra.

He came hurrying up to our table and sat heavily in his place, and then he announced to all and sundry that he had been consulting the many instruments aboard the submersible and they were telling him that the SS *Utopia* was in danger of imminent attack.

We all stared at him. The other diners at the table chuckled indulgently, knowing his reputation for high drama and outlandishness. Captain Timperley himself looked indulgently at the Professor, and Van Halfling and I exchanged a glance. We both knew that Zarathustra wasn't the kind to make idle prognostications of this sort. If he told us that we were about to be attacked, then we had better start making plans.

Zarathustra sat himself down heavily and nodded in greeting at us as the captain asked him from whom such an attack might be expected.

'As I said,' the Professor snapped churlishly, tossing a whole bread bun into his mouth, 'we are in the vicinity of an ancient undersea kingdom. The inhabitants have learned that I have discovered their whereabouts. They know I am here, aboard your ship. And so, I believe, they have sent their protectors and sentinels to attack you.' He waved the waiter over, wanting to order his food quickly.

'Sentinels? Protectors?' asked the Captain.

Zarathustra beetled his immense eyebrows at us all. 'Cephalopods, Captain Timperley.'

His meal was hurried to him, so that he could catch the rest of us up. He produced a strange, hand-held device, fashioned from cherry wood and brass. It bleeped at us and showed livid green lights which, the Professor claimed, represented the giants of the deep, come to capsize us.

I exchanged another glance with Van Halfling, who was pale with fear, but also – I believe – rather excited by the Professor's words. The same cannot be said of our companions at the captain's table. They started mocking the Professor.

I started to wonder whether it might be prudent to slip away, Nellie. Perhaps slip back to my cabin to pack a bag. Just in case. And, sure enough, as the desserts were being brought out and the waiters slipped between tables with silver platters of blancmange and trifle, the ship began to roll.

Zarathustra shrugged, 'And so it begins,' he said, clicking his fingers for jelly.

'So *what* begins?' snapped Captain Timperley crossly. Zarathustra was evidently starting to grate upon his nerves.

A steward came over, quite quickly, and whispered in the Captain's other ear. Try as I might, I couldn't make out a word of this supposedly urgent message. Then our captain was tossing aside his napkin and making his apologies to all of us around his table. He straightened up, stood, saluted us all, and was gone.

I must admit, I felt a little chill of foreboding run through me.

Another lady, a more seasoned traveller seated opposite, made some gay quip about the Captain's duties and how he could never sit still for long.

Professor Zarathustra seemed unfazed by what was transpiring. He sat there, digging into what Van Halfling had left of his steak and kidney pudding and busily ignoring the rest of us.

Even when the hullaballoo started, he hardly turned a hair. He continued to eat very energetically.

First of all, there was a scream, followed by several others, from somewhere outside the dining hall. Heads went up, and there were a few frowns of disapproval. Then came other, more distant shouts, ringing out over the noise of the band, whose tempo let up only for a moment or two.

Van Halfling caught my eye and his expression was very dark.

A ripple of frightened excitement seemed to move through the dining room then. The diners were suddenly noisier, as they put down their cutlery amid a buzz of worried conversation.

The ship lurched violently once, and then again. Chairs were overturned, trolleys were dashed against tables. Glass smashed and more screams rent through the air. The very ground beneath our feet buckled and bounced and I found myself, I'm not ashamed to admit, screaming.

I stared at the chaos as it broke out at the tables around us. This is it, I couldn't help myself from thinking: this is exactly how it was for those poor souls, last year aboard the *Titanic*. And now the same ghastly thing is going to happen to all of us as well.

The ship rocked heavily from side to side and I and everyone else at the captain's table was on their feet. All apart from Professor Zarathustra, who continued to shovel suet and gravy and jelly into his mouth as if he hadn't a care in the world. Remarkable fortitude, that man, thought I wildly. Was he taking particular relish in a final meal, as he tackled both first course and dessert together? Or was this the strange calm exhibited by a man who knows far more than his companions about what is truly going on?

Disaster brings us strange compulsions. Overtaken by the thought that we were about to meet the same fate as the *Titanic*, I found I had to run back to my cabin, in order to fling a few necessaries into my bag. I had a feeling that the worst was about to happen, and I couldn't greet it in an evening gown. And so, taking my life into my hands, I fled the table, the dining room, and hastened towards the First Class cabins, which weren't too far away. I paid no heed to Van Halfling's shouted imprecations as I tottered away.

There were shrieks from some of the lady diners. I knew for certain something awful was happening, and I had a superstitious dread of facing it without my overnight bag and good woollen coat.

'Mrs Danby!' A male voice was calling me. It was Professor Zarathustra, calling me back to my pudding. 'We must remain calm!'

But even his patrician tones were drowned out then, by the screeching of lower-class diners. I turned in time to see where everyone was looking, through the largest viewing window at the far end of the room. It was supposed to show us endless vistas of the ocean before us.

Instead, all that could be seen was the gigantic orange eye of a cephalopod. A vast octopus, Nellie. Its many limbs were wrapped tightly around the SS Utopia and its single eye filled the viewing window. It was staring straight at us!

FIVE
VAN HALFLING

from the journal of doctor abraham van halfling

THIS IS THE STORY OF THE FINAL HOURS UPON THAT DOOMED VESSEL, THE *SS Utopia*. There have been several accounts and rather wild tales about what happened that dreadful spring night but none is definitive.

It was the day that my new travelling companion – Mrs Martha Danby, late of Balcombe Street – and I made the acquaintance of that gruff and indomitable Professor Zarathustra. He is a professional thrill-seeker and self-proclaimed most brilliant man in the Empire. Ach, I have seen nothing in him so far that would lead me to describe him as brilliant. He is an arrogant and braggardly man, striding about in a too-tight safari suit and shouting at everyone through a vast black beard. He has a tiny submersible whose collision with the *Utopia* was the cause of much brouhaha the day before our ship's capsizing. I must stress that Zarathustra's craft was not the reason for said capsizing – although, as I later pointed out to Mrs Danby, it could not have done it much good, either.

No – and here I must set down the truth – the reason for the sinking of the SS *Utopia* was the giant cephalopod which rose out of the sea during first service of dinner on Thursday night. The giant octopus was joined by several of its many-limbed fellows from the depths, and between them they saw to it that the *Utopia* went down.

It was an horrific occurrence. And it was over so terribly quickly. Between the serving of the cold consommé and the final inexorable whirlpool that followed the disappearance of the ship, I would say there was less than three hours.

As with the *Titanic*, the previous year, there was a concatenation of horrible events which prevented the rescue of many of the ship's passengers. The nearest large vessel was too far away to effect a quick rescue and the messages that were sent by the *Utopia* were too garbled and incredible for anyone to take very seriously at first. Giant octopi? Really? Surely several of someone's legs were being pulled?

But in my career I have seen terrible, monstrous things. I know about the darker, stranger, more deadly creatures that walk and crawl and slither across the Earth. I had no trouble believing in the existence of these beasts, and I was the only person who didn't laugh when Professor Zarathustra told us about them at the Captain's table.

Ach, they chuckled at him – the captain and the millionaires – and even Mrs Danby gave an indulgent guffaw. But she was very struck by him, I could see. Ever since he had come aboard she had been in thrall to the swaggering brute.

I must admit, I felt I had been pushed aside by Zarathustra's advent. Mrs Danby was gasping and swooning at his every word. She quizzed him about his adventures in South America, and at the Earth's Core, and even on the Moon. I thought he was stretching credulity with that one, a little, but Mrs Danby seemed to drink every word of it in.

I remember – during the early onslaught by the colossal octopi, when we just thought the sea was being a bit choppy – how Zarathustra revealed that the ancient undersea city was said to hide a secret. An amazing secret that all the world would want to know about when he uncovered it. He had read, in some ancient text he had plundered from a Mayan tomb, how the people of that subaqueous city had distilled a perfect elixir of life. He paused impressively as he announced that he was on a mission to discover the secret of immortality!

I thought the fellow was insane, to be raving about such arcane matters while octopi of enormous proportions were in the process of wrapping their arms around the many decks of the *Utopia*. Our ship was swaying and bucking in the most alarming fashion. And yet, despite everything, something was nagging at me. A memory had stirred, deep in my mind. I, too, had read something about a city with a wonderful secret like the one Zarathustra had described. I made a rather flippant remark about how we could all do with a taste of that elixir. To my surprise Zarathustra demurred at this. He himself had no desire to be younger, and dearly longed for some kind of quiet retirement. No, he wanted to find this elixir not for himself, but for another, much more precious to him.

For myself, I am suspicious of any mention of eternal life. I narrowed my eyes at the ebullient Zarathustra, who was slurping up two courses at once with one hand, and checking a strange kind of electronic device with the other. To me, eternal life smacks too much of the filthy practices of the vampire. Ach, I will have no truck with elixirs of any kind.

Then the screaming started. Mrs Danby dashed off, away from our table, before any of us could prevent her. Strange, since she hadn't struck me as the excitable type who panics easily.

Our attention was drawn to a storm-lashed picture window, and what appeared to be a massive eye that had come level with it. The eye was peering into the dining room: a blazing, hateful orange and red, with a pupil as dark and fathomless as Hades. We all got up with alacrity and there was a chaotic few minutes as the diners ran hither and thither, stampeding towards the exits.

Zarathustra, I noticed, looked somewhat smug. 'They have come for me,' he boomed. 'They have sensed my approach and are determined to destroy me!' Our fellow diners were streaming past him, and Captain Timperley had already fled to the bridge, to see what he could do.

I had a feeling that there was nothing he could do. We were in the vicelike grip of monsters from hell. We could see the suckers on the creatures' legs against the other dining hall windows, and they looked vicious. They were never going to let us go.

Out on the decks the passengers were tearing towards the lifeboats. There was no observance of the 'women and children first' command. Not this time. Passengers of all genders and ages were jumping into the boats any old how, and it was quite clear no one was in charge.

'Luckily,' Zarathustra said, 'I have my own arrangements.'

We were witness to a dreadful sight just then. A long, whip-like tentacle rose dripping up the side of the ship as high as our present deck. It lashed itself several times around one of the half-full lifeboats. A ghastly scream went out as it pulled and dragged the boat from its fixings, dislodging several passengers, who fell screaming into the freezing sea, far below. Others clung on, and they were dragged slowly but surely into the depths several moments later.

I tore myself away from this sight and others, equally foul. Zarathustra paused before the spectacle of the massive head of one of the beasts. It had hauled itself level with the bridge, and was lashing out with a parrot-like beak, gobbling up mouthfuls of seamen and then emitting the most hideous screeching cry.

I admit I had a terrible thought just then. 'If we are all doomed to sink to the bottom of the ocean, then at least we take the ship's complement of vampires with us. They can do little harm when they are at the bottom of the sea.' But immediately I countered that prospect with the sure knowledge that they would be like ship's rats. Somehow they would sneak away and escape the ignoble end the rest of us would surely meet that night.

All except, that is, Zarathustra. He was still capering about and chuckling about how he had plans of his own.

I was distracted then by the sight of Mrs Danby, returning to the dining room. She was carrying a shoulder bag, into which she had seemingly crammed all of her valuables. She looked worried, yet was delighted to be intercepted by us as she came through the panicking crowd of First Class passengers in their finery.

I admit that I was most pleased to see her again at that moment.

'Behold, Mrs Danby!' Zarathustra pointed out the monstrous octopus in its entirety, as it clung to the command deck of the ship. Its clasp might almost have been a loving one, if one ignored the grisly death and destruction spreading in its wake. 'The Kraken of the deep wreaks its revenge on puny mankind!' Zarathustra roared, above the apocalyptic racket.

'Fancy,' said Mrs Danby, looking stricken and as if she didn't quite know what to do next. 'Should we try to get on a lifeboat, do you think?'

But that certainly wasn't Professor Zarathustra's ambition. He was far too busy shouting into the wind-whipped waves that came crashing over the sides of the deck.

'They have come for me, Mrs Danby! All of this death and destruction is because of me!'

Mrs Danby – excellent woman that she is – commented that if that was true then the Professor didn't look too bothered about the fact. Instead he seemed, rather, to take all this death and destruction as a compliment. He waggled his vast, sopping beard as if to indicate that she had hit the nail bang on the head.

'Exactly! Didn't I say that my presence was known of by the denizens of the deep?'

I looked at Mrs Danby then and saw a change come over her. Earlier that very day she had been in raptures at the hirsute dilettante's tall tales and boasts. Now it was as if she was seeing him anew. There then followed a swift debate on rationalism and likelihood, with the former housekeeper asserting that it was highly unlikely that the octopi were doing anything but pleasing their brutish selves, and Zarathustra refuting this in the strongest terms. It seemed that, whatever the circumstance, he always put himself in the very centre of the picture.

'Precisely!' he boomed. 'And now, I suggest we repair to my undersea vessel!'

Desperate as we were to survive this dreadful night, I don't think either Mrs Danby or I had entertained the idea of escaping to that unique submersible. I saw my companion's back stiffen and her eyebrows go up several notches. She was shivering in her thin evening frock, even with a woollen coat over the top, and I longed to go to her and offer her my satin-lined cape for warmth, or indeed just to put my arm around her, but I was not at all sure whether such a gesture might be welcomed.

She said hotly, 'I'm not going anywhere near your submersible!'

There could be no doubt, though, that the SS *Utopia* was doomed to sink. Already we were standing on an incline, and struggling to maintain our perpendicularity. With alarming swiftness, it seemed, the ship was succumbing to the briny, as if the combined strength of those evil-legged beasties was dragging it inexorably to hell.

Mrs Danby gave me a fierce stare and demanded that I lead her to the lifeboats, where we would join our fellow passengers and take our chances upon the surface of the sea.

Ach, I was more than ready to comply. It seemed to me that Zarathustra was not only a boastful fool. He was also a dangerous madman. What happened next proved me right.

The professor suddenly reached into his safari suit jacket and – quick as a flash – whipped out a pistol. I saw at once that it was a powerful little handgun of American manufacture. It was shiny and new, glinting in the hectic moonlight. It was quite obvious that the egocentric oaf meant business.

'I will have no compunction about using this,' he bellowed at us.

Mrs Danby almost dropped her heavy bag in alarm. 'You can't shoot us!' she cried. 'What would be the point of that?'

'Madam,' he boomed, 'my interest lies in securing your cooperation, and I will use any means to that end. Perhaps by shooting your friend in the arm, say.'

'Don't maim him!' she cried. 'That's his staking arm!'

Ach, even in my vexation and slight worry that the man might be idiotic enough to shoot me, I felt rather pleased by her alarm and concern for my personal and professional well-being.

'Then let us make our way to my transport,' he said, rather grimly, his mouth a tight, determined line in that mass of bristling beard.

As we struggled uphill towards the on-board tennis courts, all was chaos. There were screams of terror and tortured howls of buckling metal. There also came the unearthly ululations of the triumphant sea beasts as they neared the end of their grisly task.

Mrs Danby had started babbling about claustrophobia and how she couldn't possibly go underwater, in any kind of submersible. How she even felt a bit panicked when she ventured into the stair cupboard to fetch her cleaning things. But Professor Zarathustra had turned as steely as his gleaming pistol. He would brook no refusals. And so we entered the storm-lashed tennis courts, where the tiny craft was dry docked, narrowly escaping the attentions of a lashing tentacle. Zarathustra fired off several shots and the slimy appendage quickly withdrew.

And then he flung open the brass lid of his submarine and trained his pistol directly at us, his unwilling companions. 'You two are coming with me,' he growled. 'Whether you like it or not!'

To my Darling Wife, Mrs George Edward Zarathustra,

You, my dear, are no stranger to the desperate measures I am sometimes forced to adopt. And you, for one, would not be surprised at my steely-hearted determination that night upon the *SS Utopia*. It was plain that the vessel was going down, and going down rapidly. Soon it would be on the seabed, and everyone aboard it would be drowned. It was every man, woman and child for his, her and itself, and you know better than most that these are some of the conditions in which your husband comes into his own and is at his best.

All around us passengers were being helped by crewmembers into the life rafts. I had calculated – in a mere flash – that there would be enough vessels for everyone to make good their escape from that doomed bark. Lessons were learned last year following the *Titanic* disaster, and I was content that most living souls aboard would be saved. There was nothing, on the other hand, that could be done for those who met their ends in the grip of the violent giant octopi.

My two companions were keen to hurry to the lifeboats, but I had other ideas. I know you will forgive me my impetuousness, my dear, but I'm afraid I had to pull a gun on them. They looked rather shocked. In the midst of all that destruction and danger, here was one of the Empire's greatest heroes holding them at pistol point. Had I become a villain, suddenly? Driven out of my wits by fright, perhaps? As you know, I am no great admirer of firearms and only use them when I need to in order to get what I want.

I saw Mrs Danby look as if she thought me insane. Van Halfling, too, looked as if he was dealing with someone addle-pated. But why couldn't they see? I merely needed to convince them to escape from this sinking ship with me aboard my mini-submarine. There seemed no quicker way to make this plain than to whip out my pistol and tell them what to do. Of course I wouldn't kill them, as Mrs Danby thought. What would be the point of that? When I waved my gun at her pale-faced companion she gasped: 'Don't maim him! That's his staking arm!'

There was no time for such stuff and nonsense. When the chips are down there is no room for qualms or ninnying about. I waggled my weapon and motioned them to advance carefully across the perilous deck towards the storm-lashed tennis courts. There my vessel was waiting, with its lid open and all the workings within primed and ready to bear us safely away. Why couldn't these two dunderheads see that I was acting in their best interests?

Van Halfling started beseeching me, but I barely listened. I believe he wanted to see if he could help others escaping to the lifeboats. He believed he could search the lower levels for those who hadn't made it out yet. I believe it was all a pose, this heroic nonsense he started spouting just then. He was trying to attract Mrs Danby's attention, in order to distract her eyes from yours truly. I burst out at him: 'Oh, really! What could an ancient old devil like you do in the way of helping?' He looked so very frail and elderly at that moment, it was laughable.

The ship was rocking and swaying and it felt like it was going down at any moment. Even the octopi had withdrawn somewhat, as if stepping back to observe their calamitous handiwork.

I gestured fiercely at the submersible with my handgun and the two of them saw that they had no choice. It was survival or death. And, in fact, the very last of the life rafts was being launched just then, as I later heard. My submersible was the only safe way off the *Utopia* by then.

Mrs Danby took my strong paw and nimbly shinned up the ladder to the portal. She clutched her sopping wet shoulder bag to her chest and lowered herself gingerly into the machine. Van Halfling went after her, scowling darkly. I bellowed instructions as to where they were to sit and how to fasten themselves in. The gale was whipping and howling so loudly around me that I wondered if they could hear even my urgent shouting.

At the last I clambered up the side of my trusty ship and flung myself in through the single point of entry. Once inside the close confines, I slammed shut the door with an echoing, wonderful clang. That noise meant nothing less to me than complete assurance of our continued survival. Now that the three of us were sealed into my bronze sphere, we were utterly safe. Nothing could penetrate and get to us. And if we sank with the ship, then all to the good. Sinking was what the sphere was built to do.

It was dark and chilly aboard the sub. I rapped on the correct controls and the interior glowed gently, suddenly, with an amber light. I looked down into an interior of polished golden metal and mellow, polished wood, from inside of which loomed the two terrified faces of my companions. They were sitting exactly where I had instructed – Van Halfling in the second pilot's seat, to the left of the Captain's chair, and Mrs Danby in the passenger's place, behind. She seemed feverish and panicked, but determined to keep herself under control. Everything she does seems only to confirm her singularity to me. I think she is rather excellent, which I hope you won't mind me saying, my love?

They simply stared at me as I jumped off the interior ladder and strode to my Captain's chair. I swaggered – I admit it – as I squeezed into my accustomed place. Here I was: master of my destiny once again, and rescuer of two fellow adventurers.

Just then the sub gave a tremendous lurch and Mrs Danby screeched.-

'It is all right!' I cried. 'We are just in time!'

What I meant by that, of course, was that events outside were inevitably taking a turn for the worse. The *Utopia* had split in the middle, and the foremost half of the ship had slid suddenly into the freezing water. Our portion was about to go after it... at any moment, it seemed.

'Not a drop of water can get into the submersible,' I reassured them gladly. 'I hope you'll enjoy a comfortable journey.'

Van Halfling muttered something I didn't quite catch. I was busily flicking the relevant switches and turning dials, and concentrating on the array of controls that would bear us away from the scene of horror.

'You may thank me now,' I bellowed at my passengers, tossing my handgun to one side. 'For saving your lives and giving you the opportunity to make good your escape aboard the world's most miraculous creation.'

I heard something very like a snort from the sour old vampire-killer and, when I glanced round at Mrs Danby, she just looked rather scared. I put the two of them out of my head while I brought my skill to bear on the navigational controls of the sub. Although we were quite safe, we could still be shaken up and buffeted about if I wasn't careful. We needed to be guided away from the impending wreckage of the *Utopia*, into clearer and less hectic waters, if we were to remain in control of our destination. To this end I wrestled manfully with the controls just as a huge wave rolled heavily over what remained of the ship's deck and bore us away into the Atlantic. I held on tight to the steering wheel and jammed my feet to the pedals as my travelling companions screeched and howled. The sphere turned top over bottom and soon it was impossible to tell which way was up or down.

Soon we were in the ocean again and powering steadily away from the sinking ship. Still my passengers were crying out, and it was no use my shouting at them and trying to convince them that all was well. This was the element that the submersible was intended for, and all of these sensations they were experiencing were quite normal. But it was not until we had stopped rolling bottom over top and come to a much smoother descent through the waters that Danby and Van Halfling's hysterical cries died down.

'Oh my goodness, what's happening to us?' cried that remarkable lady, invoking a deity that I doubt her previous employer would have had much time for. She gripped my shoulder with surprising strength.

Van Halfling was staring at the glass portals which, several moments ago, were all white-frothed, whipped-up waters. Now, they were inkily dark, much calmer, as we drifted steadily through fathoms. 'How deep are we?' he asked, looking at me with – I saw now – rather intensely blazing eyes. I think I might have underestimated this old man, my dear. There is something in his eyes I imagine his vampiric opponents would find very disconcerting.

I explained to them both that I was taking us away from the wreckage of the *Utopia*. Though it presented no real danger to us, I still judged it best that we came out of the way. I had no real idea what would happen to my submersible if, for instance, it should be crushed into the distant seabed under the colossal mass of the sunken ship.

'You didn't care what became of the other passengers,' Mrs Danby said to me accusingly. 'You didn't care who lived or died.'

There was no use pointing out that this wasn't strictly true. She was painting a picture of me in her head: a ruthless and selfish portrait. One of a hero who is bold and utterly pragmatic, who would stop at nothing in order to save himself. I wondered whether, in addition to her undoubted concern for the other passengers, she was also rather intrigued and attracted by my tough exterior. She looked rather as if she might be. As you would have been, at that very moment, had you been there, dear wife.

Van Halfling muttered something darkly then. Something rather sardonic about how convinced I am of my superiority and my genius, and how I appear to believe I owe it to mankind to make sure that I survive any kind of disaster ahead of the common mass. All I could say in reply was, 'Well, of course! Naturally, the survival of Professor Zarathustra is paramount! The human race needs him far more than it does any number of ordinary men!'

The old man gave me a look that he clearly hoped was withering, but it wasn't. I couldn't tell if Mrs Danby was horrified or secretly impressed. I turned back to piloting us through the unknown.

These were the murky depths of a whole new underwater landscape. When I was last here, just a day before, it was a darkly peaceful land, with the blackness breaking up into brilliant colour if you looked and concentrated hard enough. Strange sea beasts came swimming up to my windows, things that I doubt anyone had ever seen before. But today the sea was mightily disturbed by the sinking ship. All other life was fleeing in the face of this calamity. It was as if a mighty airborne city was breaking up into bright fragments and dropping out of the sky.

Hm. Zarathustra is becoming poetic in his old age, my dear – forgive me. As I drew us away we saw horrid, frozen corpses turning end over end through the turbid waters. Bunk beds and billiard tables, writing desks and reclining chairs... all were useless now, sinking inevitably the several miles down into obscurity.

I didn't even ask my companions for their opinion on our next course of action. I believe they thought I would return them to the surface, just as soon as I could. But why would I do that? It was freezing up there, that cold and wet night air filled with the dying moans of those who hadn't made it to the boats. Yet, thanks to the in-built heating system which had now kicked in, we were warm and dry aboard the sub.

I gunned the engines and directed the sphere to plunge downwards into the ocean. Deeper and deeper.

'My ears are popping!' Mrs Danby shot me an accusatory look.

'We're going even deeper!' shouted Van Halfling. 'What are you doing, you madman?'

I let out a great whoop of laughter! I couldn't help it!

'To the bottom of the ocean!' I shouted at them both. 'Now is our chance to find this miraculous city at the bottom of the sea!'

My Dear Nellie,

Thanks heavens I was unable to write to you then, at that particular time. You would have feared for my very soul!

I was in the utmost turmoil. I was still in the grip of an armed madman. And I was still under the sea, in a submersible no bigger than a baker's van, and I was trapped in there with two infamous adventure-seekers.

Professor Zarathustra was acting very strangely just then. He was at the fiendishly complicated controls of his underwater craft and singing an awful song. He looked round now and then, and his eyes were gleaming with triumph. He clearly wanted me to admire him and praise his skill in getting us away from the wreckage of the *Utopia*.

But I decided that I should do no such thing. I would not encourage the impossible man. He held a gun on us, Nellie! He threatened to shoot off both of Van Halfling's arms and then his legs! Or somesuch. I had never been so alarmed in all my life. And then, on top of that, there was the ship, going down all around us, and people jumping overboard and into rafts and generally screaming and having a dreadful time.

What of Van Halfling in all of this? He had gone very quiet. He looked a little less dapper and composed than usual.

Together we stared out of a porthole at the remains of the *Utopia* floating down to the distant seabed. It was a sobering sight. It was almost graceful, the way it dropped so surely, knowing where it was going and submitting peacefully to the deep. Horrible, horrible sight. And just a few hours before we had been enjoying ourselves. Having dinner. Taking strolls. Trying not to have a care in the world.

I wondered how much air was aboard that tiny vessel. It couldn't last for ever, could it? I wondered if our host Zarathustra had even thought of that?

My ears were popping. I had a headache starting in both temples. Drilling into my brain. It might have been because I was squinting in that dull amber light through the porthole at all the horror beyond. I decided I must stop looking for a few moments.

It turned out, of course, that the build-up of pressure in my ears and behind my temples was all to do with Professor Zarathustra's decision to take us deeper down under the ocean. I hadn't realized at first, but we were plummeting fathoms deep to where no light can penetrate.

Naturally I remonstrated with the Professor, just as soon as I ascertained where we were heading. I told him in no uncertain terms that I thought we ought to be making for the surface. Man was not meant to go grubbing about on the seabed, I felt sure of it. No good would come of this impromptu expedition. And besides – I added hotly – did we or did we not have enough air to last us?

Well, Nellie, if you could have seen his face. He looked like a wounded child. A great sulky boy – though with a vast bushy beard. As if I had slapped him and tried to send him to bed with no supper.

Van Halfling – remembering his gallantry – added his voice to my protests then, and told Zarathustra than he ought to do as 'the lady' – that was me – demanded. We should return toot suite to the surface and start helping out with survivors, perhaps, or coordinating the rescue of those life rafts.

Zarathustra consulted his instruments just then, and declared that an ocean liner seemed already to be en route to the scene of the disaster. He could even pick up their radio signals as they bounced the latest news around between England and the United States. Zarathustra was in no hurry to return to the fray.

'We are tumbling into the darkest, coldest place on the Earth,' he told us. 'No one has ever penetrated so far before. Except I – last Thursday. And that is when I felt I was close to my object.'

Oh, how his dramatic voice boomed inside that submersible, Nellie. I did wish he'd pipe down.

Anyhow, the upshot was, he wanted to try out for this hidden, secret city at the bottom of the sea again. Now that we were there, it seemed, the temptation was all too much for him.

Van Halfling and I exchanged a glance, worrying that the handgun would come out again. Zarathustra was adept at getting his own way when the chips are down. We knew that we couldn't overpower him. If we did, we felt that there was no way that we could pilot that funny craft by ourselves. We were at his mercy, Nellie!

Then...

'Look! Look – out there!' Professor Zarathustra cried. He thrust one of his huge, hairy paws at the largest of the view screens. Well, all of outside was just dark murk, as far as I could tell. Drifting patches of purple and green, like mist on a nasty night in the East End, was all I could discern. But Zarathustra urged us to look harder and concentrate.

The submersible's metal hull screeched and scraped across some kind of reef of rock, and we felt ourselves swinging round and bouncing... but then we saw it,

Nellie. I couldn't deny the sight of it with my own eyes. Yes, yes! Zarathustra was right! He was actually right!

A golden glow was all I saw at first. A flash of light. Then... buildings! Dwelling places, with artificial lights inside, down here in the gloom. And far away, over the next jagged rise, a sprawling city... just as he had promised. The Professor let out a surprising yelp of joy as he clapped his eyes on the same vista as I did.

But then the submersible was wrenched around violently, and I thought we had struck another outcropping of rock. Van Halfling shouted, and gripped my arm so tightly it hurt.

Now we couldn't see the city any more. We were facing the wrong way. Something had pulled us violently away from that amazing view.

Van Halfling knew what it was straight away. Zarathustra looked peeved, and I felt alarmed. And then we all saw the limbs of the cephalopods stretching across every single porthole and screen that the little vessel possessed.

They were twisting and writhing. Our poor tiny submersible was locked inside an unbreakable grip, and I believe we all felt rather panicked at the very thought of that. Professor Zarathustra cursed and swore – quite forgetting that he had a lady on board – and he wrestled with the controls of his sub, making the engines growl like fury in a futile attempt to break free.

Van Halfling kept his cool, and you could tell that his mind was ticking over possible solutions. But it isn't a situation that you find yourself in very often, is it? And instant solutions were thin on the ground just then.

Zarathustra came to a sudden decision and clicked a few switches. With a great air of authority he turned to Van Halfling and told him that his help would be required. The vampire hunter nodded tersely, and I was impressed by his courage.

Zarathustra opened a hidden compartment and there, lying within, like hulking great bodies in a tomb, were two identical diving suits and helmets. They were gold and copper and looked like they weighed a ton each. Our pilot declared, in a tone that brooked no argument, that the two men were to don these suits and venture outside with knives and harpoons. They would engage the unfriendly sea beasts in hand to hand combat.

Though he tried to hide it, I saw Van Halfling go quite pale at this suggestion. He never wavered. He simply nodded stiffly, and started to unbutton his waistcoat. I turned away and studied the blinking control panels as my two male companions stripped to their underthings and pulled on their diving suits. My attention was caught up with the panels of controls relating to the heating and insulation of the submersible. Perhaps already a plan was being hatched within my mind. I'm not sure at which point my little moment of inspiration came, but I like to think it was starting then.

At last they were ready – and a terrifying sight they were, with their massive gauntlets and bulbous heads with dark little windows through which I could barely see their faces. They spent some moments fiddling with the tangled umbilical cords that tethered them to our oxygen supply.

Then, as if the deep-sea monsters outside realized that plans were afoot, they stepped up their fishy onslaught, exerting their limbs to rock our ship from side to side. There followed a quite terrifying few minutes, as we were struck repeatedly against the rocky reef. It felt as if our own poor bodies would be expelled into the freezing sea at any moment.

But the octopi tired themselves out soon enough, and they found that they couldn't break the vessel apart quite so easily. The water seethed outside as they thrashed around in frustration. I caught horrid glimpses of eyes and savage beaks as they peered through portholes at us. We must have looked such tasty morsels to them.

Or was Zarathustra perhaps right? Were they in fact sentinels and guardian warriors of the undersea city that we had spied? Could these creatures have as much intelligence as that?

All I could do then was watch – holding my breath (though they explained that wasn't strictly necessary) as Zarathustra opened up the airlock in order to allow the two of them to make their way out into the water. They wriggled awkwardly like newborn babes and emerged feet first into the unwelcoming atmosphere. How clumsily they grappled with their harpoons and daggers! Nellie, I could hardly bear to look. I thought the two of them would be snatched up at once by the savage octopi and devoured in a flash, metal suits and all.

Miraculously, however, the monsters didn't notice them at first. Not until the bulkier of the two – evidently Zarathustra – surged forth through the sluggish waters and prodded the closest beast with his harpoon. The creature flinched and thrashed its legs, and a dark mist of blood obscured my view almost at once. I caught odd flashes then, of a battle being fought, immediately outside the sub. I saw flailing limbs – both suckered and slender, and bulky and metallic. I saw gushing blood and squiddish ink, and the flashing blades of my two gallant protectors.

Zarathustra was clearly the more proficient at this armed hand-to-tentacle combat. Van Halfling was game but easily bested by the muscular beasts. I gasped and clutched at the ornate control panels – convinced, for a moment or two, that his suit had been ruptured by the force of a blow that had cast him aside.

But, no matter how skilled or brave my two companions were, down there in the sepulchral depths of the ocean, I suddenly saw that the outcome was horribly inevitable. The malevolent, multi-limbed fish were in their own element, and the two gentlemen were not. Though they tried their damnedest, the suits that preserved their lives were tiring them out and dragging them down. I saw at once that the cephalopods were, in fact, enjoying themselves playing a pleasant game with the two men who they fancied for their supper. They lashed out and tangled with the eminent gents. They were simply biding their time until the fellows were tired and could easily be devoured.

And then what? After they had done away with my companions?

They would come for me, wouldn't they?

So I was going to have to come up with a plan.

And quickly!

EIGHT
PROFESSOR
ZARATHUSTRA

To my Darling Mrs George Edward Zarathustra,

What an excellent woman!

You know, my dear, that I am sceptical about the bravery and 'mental capacity' of womankind. Especially when the chips are down and danger rears its ghastly head. I am too often tempted to think that ladies are no good in crises, despite evidence to the contrary I have gleaned from my thirty years married to you. Still I tend to assume that members of the fairer sex are inclined to panic and go to pieces.

However, in my moment of most awful need, the astonishing Mrs Danby devised a plan upon the instant that took my breath away. It also nearly boiled both Van Halfling and me alive, but that is by the by. She saved our lives and ended those of our attackers – so hurrah for her! A jewel among her sex, as it were.

Even I had to admit that the octopi seemed indefatigable. Van Halfling – who must be seventy if he's a day – was flagging considerably, waving a harpoon gun around quite ineffectually.

Once, I spied Mrs Danby's worried face at a portal. What would become of that poor, rather plain, woman, if we two gentleman failed in our mission and died out here at the bottom of the sea?

However, it was that resourceful domestic servant who, in the end, saved us all. Somehow she cudgelled her feminine brains and realized that she could utilize the submersible itself to defeat our undersea nemeses. Her eyes turned to the control panels in front of her and lit fortuitously upon the dials that controlled the temperature of the inner and outer skins of the vehicle. Naturally my invention is equipped with its own internalized, pressurized, steam-driven heating system. How else could I hope to plumb the frigid depths of the world's oceans?

Now, the excellent Mrs Danby saw these controls and noticed that the thermostats were throbbing away and warming the interior of the sub quite nicely. What if... she must have thought... What if I turned the dials right up to the very highest settings? And what if I heated up the exterior of the craft as well? She knew – from her daily labours as cook and housekeeper – rather a lot about the conduction of heat and the uses of hot steam. And so she turned that domestic knowledge to the advantage of us all. On went the switches! Round went the dials! She barely gave herself pause to have doubts. The sweat began running freely at once. That poor lady glowed, perspired and sweated like a horse as the interior of the sub quickly started to overheat. She turned the hue of lobster thermidor before her efforts had any appreciable effect on the beings outside.

The first I knew of it, the umbilicus tethering Van Halfling and I to the sub turned hot. Soon my lungs were scorching and I was feeling rather clammy all over. Van Halfling shot me a look of alarm through his visor and before I could think further, I became aware of the effect that this over-heating was having upon our assailants.

They were being scalded!

All the while, as they had tangled with us, the octopi had left several of their limbs still wrapped securely around the sub. Now, with Mrs Danby's flash of inspiration, they found themselves and their suckers welded and melting against the metal hull. Mrs Danby was *cooking* the murderous beggars!

How I wished I could smell them, sizzling away. I chortled at the sight of it. I guffawed – despite my discomfort – at the opaque and doomed look that came into their horrible eyes.

Oh, Mrs Danby! What a genius is she! Van Halfling and I capered happily as all five of our attackers were broiled and blackened and fell from our ship and our exhausted selves. We had triumphed!

Then we had to wave frantically at Mrs Danby, to get her to turn the gauges back down. Otherwise we two would be cooked as well, which would have been very counter-productive. In a lather of sweat and self-congratulation, she grappled with the controls, and then set about finding the correct way to open the airlock and re-admit us to the sub.

Oh, dear Mrs George Herbert Zarathustra. Imagine our glee! Just picture our ruddy complexions as we clambered back inside my tiny sub and stripped off our metal armour. It was still too hot, almost to touch. Van Halfling and I were hopping about in our undergarments, singed and bruised and too excited for words. It was the first time I had seen the old man shaken out of his impeccable calm. He was prancing about in jubilation, ecstatic to be alive. Poor Mrs Danby was flustered and damp, laughing as the pair of us gathered her up in a hug.

Most unseemly behaviour! I am sure you will agree, my darling wife. But who is to say what modus is appropriate in such unique circumstances? Who else in the history of mankind has weathered such bizarre calamities – and gigantic calamari – and come out quite unscathed at the other end? Why, only Zarathustra and Company!

Oh, possibly that rapscallion Captain Zero, too. He's probably encountered such things as well, but that's a story for another day, as they say.

But here we were – overly hot and overtired – and glad to be alive. Imagine, taking a steam bath at the bottom of the ocean! My very eyeballs felt as if they were being poached like eggs. I had the most marvellous idea then, and flung open the mini-bar, which was sequestered behind an oak panel, revealing several bottles of champagne on ice. We took the ice and rubbed it all over ourselves in order to cool down, and then Mrs Danby opened all the bottles in quick succession. The noise of popping corks was most welcome, though she was careful where they shot off in the confined space.

And so – before we faced our next challenge – I am afraid we three adventurers became rather tiddly.

Which might go some way to explaining the shocking and regrettable behaviour that followed. I am sorry to say that before the end of that very hour, the three of us had had something of a noisy and violent contretemps.

It's no good – I can't skip over this most lamentable portion of my tale. I must proceed and relate to you how I disgraced myself – though I did it, naturally, only with the best intentions, and in the cause of science and knowledge, naturally.

It was some minutes after our celebratory noise had died down and we were draining the third bottle of champers. Normally, as you know, I hardly touch of drop of alcohol, but we certainly felt that we deserved it. Perhaps it wasn't a good idea to indulge in the bubbly at the extraordinary pressures and in the sweltering heat of our current position? Anyhow, those tiny, invidious bubbles got into my bloodstream and made their way to my brains, where they played havoc.

Suddenly, I was on my feet and swaying.

'The lost city!' I was shouting. 'The city lies just over those rocky crags! I have searched for it for years. Everything has built up to this moment! And now – now we can explore!'

I noticed my two companions exchange a befuddled, worried glance. But with no further ado I flung myself into the pilot's seat and started wrestling manfully with the controls. The engines whined in protest. There came a great clunking noise from somewhere in the tortured apparatus. Van Halfling and Mrs Danby were on their feet, standing at my back, and shouting over the groans from the machine.

'Stop this at once!' Jones's housekeeper demanded, in a tone I bet she never used with the Balcombe Street Detective. 'You'll murder us!'

'Zarathustra, listen to her,' said Van Halfling, his old, worried self again. 'You'll rupture the craft. Ach, can't you hear the mechanisms? The submersible is damaged. After the octopi and the overheating of the thermostats, we must return to the surface as quickly as possible.'

'What?!' I bellowed. 'How can you suggest such a thing? When we are so close to the city? The golden underwater city?'

Mrs Danby placed a hand on my arm. 'It'll still be there in a hundred years,' she said, thinking she was sounding wise. But I shrugged her off. Platitudes! Ninnyish caution!

'Never!' I cried, and reapplied my efforts to the controls, waggling the gearstick with abandon. 'I will force this ship to do my bidding! It will perform as I command – as its creator! And you two old women will go and strap yourselves into your seats at once!'

Again there came the horrendous racket of the engines moaning in complaint. My poor little bark! What was I thinking of, to torture it like this? But my fevered mind was possessed by the thought of cresting those tall rocks and flying into the valley beyond – and coming to land outside that vast dome covering the city we had glimpsed...

I was a man obsessed. As you know, Mrs Zarathustra, I've fallen prey before to my ungovernable passions.

'Stop! Stop!' cried Mrs Danby. 'You'll crash and murder us all!'

'Can't you hear, man?' shouted Van Halfling. 'You'll rupture her sides! She'll go off with a bang!'

'I don't care! I don't care!' I heard myself howl, and plunged onwards, heedlessly, and... for a few moments, it felt as if we were going to make it. I would be vindicated!

But then the two of them had seized me. They plied their pitiable strength against mine, hanging on to one arm each. They are two skinny little items, and no match for Zarathustra's brute strength, of course, yet they impeded my efforts to master the controls. As I tried to struggle free, I lost all purchase and the submersible began a crazy, corkscrewing motion through the black waters. We were thrown together and were bashed about terribly – and then there came the most awful bang..!

The lights went out. I was lying on the floor, or possibly the ceiling. tangled in the limbs of my two companions. They were unconscious, I thought, and I scrambled to my feet in order to seize the advantage.

As I settled myself back in the pilot's seat I realized that my precious vehicle had suffered terrible damage. Water was leaking from the portals and the viewing screens. There was an ominous hissing from the heating systems. But I managed to regain command of the steering wheel.

All I could think about was that I had poured my entire fortune into making this machine. Everything that you and I ever had went into this plan. I could never afford to build its like again. So it was now or never. I had to use every last iota of my strength and wring every drop of usefulness out of this vessel. If I wanted to see this undersea kingdom – then I had to get us there right now. This very second. Even if my two friends counselled against it in the strongest possible terms. They were simply frightened. They were ordinary human beings, overwhelmed by the dangers in which they found themselves.

'Please,' gasped Mrs Danby from the floor. 'You have to see sense, you silly man. We're running out of air! You're going to kill us all!'

But Professor George Edward Zarathustra is no ordinary human being! As you well know, my darling wife! And no matter what the cost, I was determined to succeed in my mission. I would let absolutely nothing stand in my way!

And so, as Danby and Van Halfling roused themselves, I put my foot on the accelerator and knocked them down again. We were heading for the lost city and nothing at all was going to stop me now!

NINE
VAN HALFLING

from the journal of doctor abraham van halfling

PROFESSOR ZARATHUSTRA SEEMED TO CARE LITTLE FOR THE FATES OF HIS FELLOW human beings. His main concern was preserving his own life – for the sake of the advancement of mankind, he had the gall to inform us. He also told us we were to come with him on an impromptu exploration of the ocean floor where he reckoned there lay an ancient, lost city.

So began the most perilous part of our adventure thus far with the perfidious lunatic known as George Edward Zarathustra.

I am quite used, in my line of work, to crawling through tombs and catacombs. The dark and cloistered nooks and crannies of the world hold few fears for me, but there was indeed something oppressive about questing down through the Stygian depths aboard this craft that was – as Zarathustra rightly estimated – no bigger than a bean can.

In fact, it was almost a relief when we found that we had to go outside. This was during our hair-raising battle with the octopi who had, of course, decided to pursue us deep underwater, and wrap their deadly limbs around our ship. Zarathustra claimed that they were the guardians of the lost city and, I must say, I thought there might be some truth in that. They revealed their leggy selves once more, just after we had spied that golden city.

How we celebrated when the danger was over and the two of us fellows were back aboard! Champagne appeared and drink was taken, though we were so happy, I don't think Mrs Danby or I were aware how drunk the grizzled Professor was becoming. He was dancing about in a large pair of underpants, singing of our triumph at the top of his voice. That is what he was doing one moment. The next he was possessed like a madman, and back at the controls of his submarine.

Mrs Danby and I were horrified and tried to restrain him. He was gunning the engines and firing them up. He announced that he was taking us all to the lost city immediately. Even as we tried to remonstrate with him – and to make him see that we were running out of air, and that the engines were damaged by the overheating – the crazed fellow would not listen. He was pulling the controls about rather wildly, and telling us that nothing would stand in his way this time.

Ach, you see? Neurotic, as well. He is so caught up in this fantasy of himself as the world's greatest hero and genius that his behaviour is atrocious. He will go to any lengths to prove to those around him that he matches up to that impossible vision of his own self.

Already Mrs Danby was starting to gasp and choke. We were flung to the floor and found that the metal grilles underfoot were stingingly hot to the touch. If Zarathustra didn't desist, we would be boiled like puddings inside a tin.

There really was nothing for it. I would have to take drastic measures. A cold, hard, determined feeling came over me, as it always does in moments such as these. I felt about inside my velvet smoking jacket (which had been slung to the floor, in all the tumult) and withdrew a handful of stakes. Good, hard stakes made out of oak.

Mrs Danby saw what I was doing – from her vantage point on the floor – and she looked shocked. Her eyes almost came out of her head. Her lovely, kindly eyes. I saw at once that she believed I thought Zarathustra was a vampire and under some kind of demonic possession. But no, I didn't. I didn't think that at all. All I wanted was some kind of weapon and the stakes came first and most easily to hand.

It would have been easier for me to deal with him, had he been one of the legions of the undead. At least I know where I am with those. But Zarathustra was an arrogant egotist, and they are often much harder to manage.

I stood up slowly, on trembling legs, swaying as the submersible careened madly about. I hefted a handful of stakes and stood right behind the hunched form of Zarathustra, who was intent and ranting to himself about ancient civilizations and brave explorers and some such. Then I brought down the whole handful of hardwood down upon his head. I made sure the pointy ends were facing away from him. I didn't want to kill him, just put him out of action. And they did the job. As soon as they knocked him hard on the bonce, he stiffened, groaned, and fell face forwards onto his dashboard.

Mrs Danby cheered – and went into a choking fit due to lack of oxygen.

'We'd better seize control of the submersible craft and take her back up to the surface!' I said, manhandling the bulky form of Zarathustra out of the pilot's seat.

Still coughing, and turning a delicate shade of mauve, Mrs Danby nodded in agreement.

Then I turned to the busily blinking and chaotic control panels, and sat myself down in Zarathustra's rather warm chair. Now, the thing was... where did I even start?

Mechanical and intellectual problems have never bothered me for long, however. Our quandaries are much easier to overcome if we see them simply as a serious of puzzles with which we must rigorously engage. I was trying to explain this to Mrs Danby as I surveyed the controls, and used logic to ascertain which levers and switches did what. Mrs Danby didn't seem – just at that moment – terribly interested in my discourse, and she said something about saving the air by not talking. I quite agreed with her, and elected to save my thoughts for a later airing.

Zarathustra lay face down on the hot metal floor and I tried not to think of the violence I had been forced to wreak. I was sure that, had he had his own way, the old man would have killed us all. His heart was in the right place, but he wasn't averse to taking the wildest risks. Also I think, in recent years, he has probably gone rather insane. This was my considered opinion after spending several busy hours with the gentleman.

I could tell that Mrs Danby was less enamoured of him than she had been before. I was obscurely pleased by this.

Then I managed to get the controls to respond to my careful probing. Was it my imagination, or did the submersible give a kind of relieved groan as it came under my control? No longer would it be forced to submit to its true master's demands. It didn't have to strain and shake itself apart in pursuit of a crazy dream. I was coaxing it gently to return us to the surface, many leagues above, and the sub's controls seemed to long to do that very thing. Or perhaps I am being fanciful? Ach, all I knew was that its many gold and scarlet lights twinkled at me – almost appreciatively as my hands roved over the switches and dials.

Then we began to rise. Slowly at first, but steadily. We were ascending from the gloomy deeps. And, even more incredibly, the temperature was starting to drop, as the submersible's fans sprang into action, and tried to make its occupants more comfortable.

Mrs Danby sank into her padded chair as I activated the emergency oxygen supplies and the airflow started pumping once more. She moaned softly. I turned to see her fanning herself.

'You will certainly have a tale to tell your sister,' I said to her. 'And all your other loved ones at home.' She had told me a little about her sister and her life at home in England, back aboard the SS *Utopia*. Those days and conversations aboard that luxury liner seemed to belong now to a long-lost and golden halcyon age.

'I don't think Nellie nor anyone else would believe a word of it,' she said, gaspingly. 'Perhaps we had better keep some of the details of our escapades quiet, hmm? Those details to do with the lost city we glimpsed. And the rather more regrettable aspects of Professor Zarathustra's behaviour?'

I nodded eagerly, rather surprised that she should be keen to protect the old devil. He had almost, after all, been responsible for our deaths. But there was a compassion in Mrs Danby that surpassed all else. She was capable of such magnanimous, selfless gestures – as I was about to find out – even in the case of dreadful old reprobates like George Edward, still supine as he was on the floor.

It was at this point that I – full of admiration for the courageous lady – chanced my arm. What did I have to lose? If deadly danger teaches us anything, it is to seize our chances of happiness whenever we can.

'Dear lady,' I said to her. 'When we finally arrive in the United States, at the end of this terrible affair, will you be staying long in New York City?'

She looked at me curiously, as if she hadn't until that moment seriously considered that she would live to see dry land again. 'Why yes,' she said. 'I am spending two weeks at a hotel on Seventh Avenue, rather close to Central Park.'

'Excellent,' I said. 'For I have several days in hand, before I must take the train to Philadelphia and begin on my lecture tour. I wonder if...' Ach, then I had to turn to attend to the control panel, which had started to blink and flash alarmingly. It seemed it was not to be plain-sailing surface-ward, after all!

'Yes?' she asked eagerly. 'You wonder what?'

'Perhaps we could meet for supper? At my hotel – the Algonquin. It is only a few blocks from your own.'

'Oh!' she said, and I couldn't tell if her expostulation was to do with pleasure or surprise at the way the whole submersible was starting to judder.

'We might talk over our recent adventures and toast each other's good health,' I suggested, flipping switches madly and trying to regain control of the ailing craft. 'And we might share a fond chuckle over how lucky we will both feel to be alive.'

'Indeed,' she said, and her voice was even more throaty and gasping than before. She dropped her shoulder bag to the floor as she said, 'That sounds like a marvellous idea...' And she slid to the floor, unconscious from oxygen deprivation.

I checked the overheated gauge. All of a sudden, supper at the Algonquin hotel seemed like a hopeless impossibility. We were still rather deep down underwater. Several hundred leagues, in fact, and almost completely out of air. The pressure seemed to make the very air quiver. The submersible itself was about to crack apart!

My Darling Mrs George Edward Zarathustra,

I hope you will be as horrified as I was to learn that they had betrayed me!

I came to some while later and I found that we were no longer several thousand leagues under the sea. Oh no, indeed! The cowardly quislings had not only knocked me unconscious with a terrible bonk on the noggin, but they had also somehow mastered the controls of my poor submersible and dragged us up to the surface!

All my dreams of exploring and conquering that subaqueous city were up in flames! That was an end to it, I knew it plainly at once! When I woke up – rather sorely – on the floor of my ship – I could hear the dreadful tortured notes that her engines were playing. I was witness to the ghastly music of her imminent demise! Oh, she had been handled roughly by those two skinny turncoats. They had ruined her and driven her to the very edge of her capabilities and beyond, simply in order to save their own rotten hides.

And now my poor miniature submersible was on her last legs, limping to the surface and the daylight.

All of this, I knew at once, as my consciousness returned and I heard Van Halfling and Mrs Danby fussing and gossiping over the wrecked controls. My colossal intellect struggled not at all to update itself with the events that must have transpired during my period of absence. I knew I was betrayed, and precisely what they had done.

And in that moment I vowed that somehow – by fair means or foul – I would get myself back to that undersea city. I would have my chance to plunge into its virginal depths, as it were. Even if it meant I had to resort to necromantic or magical means, the secrets of that lost metropolis would soon be Zarathustra's!

Mrs Danby exclaimed then, as she noticed that I was awake once more. She seemed alarmed and rather wary as I clambered to my feet and demanded to know who had hit me with such force I had been robbed of my wits.

She confessed gabblingly that it had been Van Halfling, who had smacked me hard with a handful of the stakes he usually utilised to slay vampires. He had, of course, kept the pointed ends away from me, which she seemed to think I ought to find some consolation. Then the two of them started flapping on about how I had become a crazed and dangerously obsessed man, risking all our lives and heading for the city.

'Of course I would have risked our lives in the pursuit of knowledge! For the Elixir of eternal life...!' I boomed – feeling rather irked. But it seems that my companions were more interested in saving their own souls.

'Oh, we've had a terrible time,' said Mrs Danby – in her common accents. 'We both passed out, you know – from all of the pressure and the violence of all the shuddering and juddering your submersible was doing. But, somehow, Doctor Van Halfling had – in the final few seconds before his consciousness blacked out – set the controls aright. And, even with us all sleeping the sleep of babes on the floor, the underwater vessel managed to get us to the surface. Out we popped!

Like a cork from out of a bottle!'

Well, bully for us, I thought, glowering hotly at them both. What is the use of surviving if you haven't done anything? If you're just limping along from one calamity to another and not actually accomplishing anything?

Well, then I turned to the controls of my beloved sub and heard them groaning and whining. I stared at the display screens as they faded and at last blinked out. It was as if the very soul of that poor craft was dying away at the touch of my fingers. It had waited until its master was awake again before expiring like this. I trembled and could barely suppress a tear at its passing. You know that I am not sentimental, wife, and so you will realise how deeply I felt in this moment for the machine I had designed and built from scratch.

I cried also because I was now not only without my own personal submarine, I was effectively penniless as well.

I turned to Mrs Danby and Van Halfling and could have banged their silly heads together. But they looked so glad to be alive that I held back – for now.

Then we were bobbing along on the brilliant surface of the North Atlantic in the full, frosty glare of the morning sunlight. Even I had to dispel the gloom that clung to me as we faced that marvellous light. I squeezed the last few droplets of use out of the radio and contacted the ocean liner that had been responsible for picking up survivors from the SS Utopia in the night. The SS Asgaard was astonished and delighted to receive a crackling, hissing message from the greatest scientist-adventurer of his age. With all due dispatch they swerved around and travelled out of their way to pick us up.

We unscrewed the lid of the submersible and the three of us hung out of the top, taking full advantage of the abundance of oxygen outside as we awaited our rescue. A glorious breeze plucked up and we cheered and sang songs and even I had to admit it had been rather stuffy and confining in the poor old sub.

Then, only an hour or so after our message had been received, the Asgaard was glimmering on our horizon. It shimmered as it approached and we cheered some more, waving as hard as we could. We tried not to notice the few bits of broken flotsam and tragic jetsam from the *Utopia* that occasionally drifted by. We saw no bodies, thank goodness.

Mrs Danby fell against my shoulder, just about fainting with happiness. 'I never thought I'd live to see dry land again,' she said.

Van Halfling – with his usual dry, gloomy wit – reminded her that she hadn't seen it *yet*.

Then the *Asgaard* was right in front of us. A magnificent vessel – even taller and more splendid than the one that the octopi had doomed. Then, for the second time in almost as many days, I was climbing hand over hand up a rope ladder to the uppermost deck of a vast ship. The lady and the vampire hunter went ahead of me, rather tremblingly and slowly, and I took the opportunity to clear out all my most vital equipment from the sub and stow it in a knapsack.

If the sailors aloft thought it strange that all three of us were emerging from the submersible in our undergarments, they were too polite to say so. And we weren't about to tell all just yet.

When I clambered out of my sub I felt so sad, as if I was leaving part of myself behind. I knew that I would never go sailing in her ever again. Once aboard the *Asgaard* I made arrangements that she be hauled out of the ocean and placed in storage. I felt sure that one of the great museums of the world would be interested in her and I might be able to find her a suitable home.

Then the captain of the *Asgaard* appeared on the deck and, after our greetings, introductions and some quick explanations, he suggested that we be given warm blankets and hot soup in the area where the other survivors were being tended. And following this, he suggested that a swift debriefing might be in good order.

MY DEAR WIFE, THEY WOULDN'T BELIEVE A WORD OF IT!

Can you credit it?

Well, I suppose you can. You have been there, haven't you, when the reasonable and the rational world of the established order have listened to Zarathustra's tales and then roundly dismissed them as hogwash. How many times has this happened to me? After the various occasions in the past I should know better, perhaps, and not expect to be believed at first. Just look at the affair of the day that everyone on Earth apart from ourselves died for several hours and then returned to life! Or the journey I undertook to South America to find creatures neglected by time itself! Or the expedition I made into the Afterlife to prove the persistence of the existence of the human soul! They laughed in my face until I could produce some kind of tangible proof. Tangible, pah! What about the conviction of an incorrigible proposition? What about knowing things with our intellect alone, eh?

Our interview with Captain Danby of the SS *Asgaard* was no different, I am afraid, to those I have endured with other pettifogging bureaucrats. No matter how I fulminated and ejaculated and expostulated at him, he wouldn't believe a word about the undersea city I had found. He had evidence and eye witness accounts for the giant sea monsters that had destroyed the *Utopia*. Why, he had even seen photographs of those, and they had by now graced the covers of daily newspapers on several continents. Giant cephalopods he could gladly swallow. But not my contention that they were being used as sentinels and guards from a hidden world beneath.

Even Mrs Danby and Van Halfling couldn't convince him. Their testimonies were listened to politely, and then dismissed as thoroughly as were mine. I felt myself grow scarlet and on the point of exploding, there and then in his office.

Captain Danby himself grew terribly cross with us. His concern was for those passengers and crew of the SS *Utopia* who had tragically met their ends that night. Over three hundred bodies were missing and presumed dead. I am afraid that he took my cool, scientific demeanour for callousness, my dear, and professed to be disgusted by my lack of human compassion. Perhaps I should never have told him that the city of gold was more important than a few drowned travellers.

But, of course, in the massive scheme of things – in the whole tumultuous sweep of human history – the discovery of this city is far more important! If only other people could see that. What if there really is such a thing as an Elixir of eternal life?

I would make sure it was given to you, first of all, my dear. How would you feel about being Mrs George Edward Zarathustra in perpetuity?

Our interview with the captain was at an end and we were shown to cabins that we might occupy for the short remainder of the journey. We were treated well and given fresh clothing to wear. We were introduced to various other survivors from the *Utopia*, but by them we were regarded strangely, and by some, almost suspiciously. Myself most of all. It was as if word had gone round that I had summonsed those slimy behemoths from the seabed myself!

I was rather lonely for the final day of our journey. Mrs Martha Danby and Van Halfling were avoiding intercourse with me. They were even avoiding it with each other. It was as if the terrifying proximity of our undersea adventure had proved too much, and now they needed space and time by themselves. Well, the *SS Asgaard* is a huge vessel and, even though we shared a suite, we didn't trouble each other with unwanted conversations. For myself, I'd have relished a chance to stew over our recent escapades.

As we approached New York harbour, small boats and tenders came out to meet us. There were shouts and congratulations and a very warm welcome for the survivors, myself included. Journalists came rushing aboard, eager to get the scoops and witnesses' accounts first for their papers. Van Halfling hid himself away. Mrs Danby seemed to relish the prospect of being flattered and cajoled into telling her tale by these spry young gentlemen. I saw them in the afternoon tearooms, agog at her stories. She was like an elderly Scheherazade of the servant class.

I longed to tell them my own tale, but something held me back. Some feeling, perhaps, that my adventure was by no means over. I did not feel ready yet to appear before the world, telling them all about my astonishing findings. Can you credit it, my dear? Zarathustra was almost demure as the land came in sight.

We rounded the headland and there was Lady Liberty, beckoning to us. And the hazy, shimmering immensity of those tall buildings of glass and steel. Oh, Mrs Zarathustra – I experienced a kind of wild surmise when I looked out at New York City from the top deck of the *Asgaard*!

I knew my destiny was bound up in her. And that there, in the heart of that city, I was to find the most bizarre and quite unscientific means with which to continue my quest. There was something waiting for me there. I could almost scent it on the air, in the turmoil of aromas that the great city breathed out. Somewhere deep inside Chinatown there was a certain magical place possessed of amazing properties and it was waiting for me. I had heard the rumours, and now I was going to pursue them, no matter what dangers lay ahead! Somehow I was determined that the City Beneath the Ocean would soon be within my grasp!

But what was this? As we prepared to disembark? On the gangplank, where I was expecting a hearty cheer as I stepped once again upon American soil. Where I was surely entitled to expect a hero's welcome.

'We have a warrant for your arrest, sir.'

There were policemen waiting for me at the dock! And they both had guns aimed at me! At Professor Zarathustra! As if he were no better than a common criminal!

ELEVEN
MRS DANBY

My Dearest Nellie,

At last, here I was. Safe and sound and on stable ground. They tell me that Manhattan island is built upon solid granite, and that is why they can erect such impressive skyscrapers on top of it. I was very glad to have rock-solid ground beneath my feet, after all my recent trials and tribulations.

I was soon installed in my luxury hotel room, on the seventeenth floor of the Wellington, on 7th Avenue. At first I didn't go out much. I was catching up with my sleep and trying to avoid the gentlemen of the press.

I made sure I sent a telegram to you, my dear sister, to let you know that I was safe and well. I imagined that you have already seen some lurid and terrifying headlines. That the tale of our adventures at sea had flashed across the globe was a fact of which I was well aware.

I saw a headline. *The New York Times* was brought in with my breakfast one morning. And there it was, on the front page.

'Great Detective's Retired Landlady Does Battle with Sea Monsters with Bare Hands While Surviving Worst Atlantic Disaster Since the *Titanic*.'

Oh, my dear Nellie. I was so ashamed. I never wanted this. I really didn't want any publicity or hoo-ha upon my entrance into the United States. As you well know, I came here for a relaxing holiday. A private trip of a lifetime. I had no desire whatsoever to be part of a circus. Or to have frankly horrifying adventures.

Anyhow – at that point I was still not fully recovered from my ordeal. Exhausted and emotionally sapped: though luckily no other worse kind of physical or mental damage had been wrought. I simply wanted to sit up in my sumptuous bed and start to pull together my thoughts in the form of a letter to you, my darling sister, to let you know that I was here. I wanted to give you the full details about what went on aboard the *SS Utopia* and in Professor Zarathustra's tiny submersible this week in the middle of the Atlantic. However, the task seemed to be monumental and my energy failed me. I found I could not pen that full and frank account just then.

Suffice to say that I wanted to put that dreadful series of events behind me, and fix my thoughts upon the future. I had a holiday to take! And a whole, marvellous city to explore! I had seen but a tiny portion of New York so far, only what could be glimpsed from the cab as I huddled under a horse blanket on my way uptown from the docks. I saw a dreadful photograph of me in *The Times*, looking the very image of a refugee in a borrowed skirt and ill-fitting blouse. I dearly hoped my former employer hadn't seen it and thought I was purposefully drawing attention to myself.

WITHIN A FEW QUIET DAYS OF SECLUSION, YOU WILL BE RELIEVED TO HEAR, I was feeling much more lively and more myself. My energy reserves had been replenished and no longer – when I closed my eyes – did I see the dreadfully dark deeps at the bottom of the ocean. Some sensible food and some long hours of sleep had done me good, and I was ready to face the world once more.

I dressed myself up as best I could in my borrowed clothes. I realized I would have to do some shopping as soon as I could, since my entire holiday wardrobe was languishing on the seabed. (Oh, I could hardly bear to think about it. All that money! All that care I took in choosing just the right things for myself!) I would need a new woollen coat (mine was destroyed in the overheating submersible) and a warm hat, for I'd heard that no matter how sunny it is in Manhattan, the wind round the sharp corners of the city blocks can cut like a knife. I would also need to visit a bank, of course. I had been told that our Embassy would help me with all my needs and wants, of course. Papers and money to tide me over and so on. But the very thought sorting all that out gave me a headache just at that moment. I still needed to acclimatize myself and leave my room under my own steam. And so I prepared myself mentally to fling myself upon this city – and went down in the lift.

Downstairs the lobby was all carpeted in scarlet and the walls were mirrored and trimmed with gold. Plush is the word I am groping for, Nellie. There was a hush. A respectful hush that felt very calming to me. I drifted over to the reception desk, where the man was togged out in the most elegant little outfit with polished brass buttons and a cap. I asked whether there had been any messages left for me, and that was when I received your wires and messages, dear Nellie. I read them quickly, pleased that you knew I was safe, and experienced a little pang of homesickness. I did wonder, though, dear, at your spending quite so much per word on a telegram in order to keep me up to date with the details of your romantic life. Surely a letter might have done?

There were other notes and letters and wires, too. At first I wasn't sure whether they were meant for me at all. They all seemed to come from strangers. I paused in my reading, peering over my spectacles at the receptionist. 'Are you sure these are mine?'

He nodded and grinned. He explained that I was still the talk of all Manhattan. The lady who had voyaged to the bottom of the sea.

'Inadvertently, I assure you,' I said crisply. 'I am not an habitual adventurer. I was kidnapped! I was shanghaied by that foolish Professor Zarathustra!'

The young man shrugged and grinned at me. He said that people loved me, nevertheless.

'Love me?' I frowned. 'How on Earth can they love me, when they don't have a clue who I am?'

'Hey, lady, you did something extraordinary,' he said, in much too familiar a tone. 'And people want to know about that. They wanna buy into that. They wanna know all about you.'

I was most perplexed, Nellie. I wasn't sure I liked the sound of that at all. In fact, as I stood at the reception desk, leafing through those various unasked-for messages, I realized that I was drawing glances from other guests and members of the public passing through the hotel lobby. Oh, my goodness. Possibly they recognized me from that dreadful photo on the front of *The New York Times*. Well, this really wasn't good enough. I didn't want attention from all these people!

'Look on the bright side,' said the young man. 'There's money to be made from an ordeal like yours. People will want the low-down.'

I frowned. 'The low-down?'

'The story from your point of view,' he offered.

I nipped this perplexing conversation in the bud and asked him for directions to Central Park. I felt like a nice, brisk walk in the open air might do me some good. The room was starting to whirl slightly. He obliged and I found that that huge area of cultivated parkland was only a very few blocks to the north. I thanked him and ventured out. The streets out there were noisy and confusing, with horses and carriages clattering and motor vehicles honking and shunting past. Soon I was in the calmer and verdant seclusion of the park, however. Birdsong and leafy branches nodding above me. I wandered for a while, consulting a tiny map in my guidebook so that I would not become lost.

Soon I found a bench by a small kind of lake affair and sat down gratefully. I felt myself immediately relax. It was rather like sitting in Regent's Park in London, not very far from Balcombe Street, what with the ducks making their racket and the chuckling fountain and the great swaying and swishing of the leafy boughs overhead. I could almost have been back there, on my afternoon break from 221B. When I opened my eyes, however, they encountered the startling sight of those grey, silver and pale brown towers spaced out like giant sentinels all around the park's perimeter. They were like vast castles in the sky, hemming me in. I am here, Nellie. I really am here. In New York City. Just as I planned to be. And quite alone.

At this point I fetched out of my handbag that pile of messages the desk clerk had taken from my pigeonhole and given to me. All these strangers! Writing with such familiarity! Praising me, extolling my virtues and bravery and fortitude. Some of them asking rather impertinent questions. I was astonished, Nellie. These Americans seem like quite a different breed. They don't stand on the same kind of ceremony as we do. And yet they are so friendly... why, you only had to look at some of the invitations I received to see that!

Oh, yes. I received invitations. I was asked out for afternoon tea and dinner and something called brunch. I was asked to talk to Ladies' societies and university students. My presence was respectfully requested at salons and meet-and-greets and parties-of-the-season.

As I read and leafed through these elaborate, gilt-edged cards I felt rather less annoyed. I was starting to feel intrigued and pleased. Why, I thought, this is society. Society itself seemed to be opening up its arms to me. I was being invited to go places, Nellie! I would be mixing with the great and the good!

OF COURSE, IT ALL BECAME RATHER OVERWHELMING AFTER A WHILE. NOT JUST those ardent requests and invitations, but also the hectic city all about me. I was sitting on my bench by the duck pond, minding my own business, and one or two people seemed to recognize me. They grinned at me and one couple even asked me if I was the famous Mrs Danby. Well, I didn't know where to look. If I had been in my right wits the other day, when I was brought ashore at the docks, I'd have refused to say anything to the press. I should never even have given them my name. I certainly shouldn't have gibbered out all those details about giant octopi and Professor Zarathustra's futuristic equipment.

Still, what's done is done and, as Doctor Wilson used to say, news today wraps fish suppers tomorrow. I would be a nine-day wonder here in New York – though nine days seemed rather a long time. Still, there were benefits. After I left the park I sauntered back down Seventh Avenue towards my hotel, thinking I would find some kind of eatery because, now that I thought on, I was ravenous. Happening into a kind of café, I was presented with a mammoth sandwich, consisting of layers of salad and greasy meat. A hamburger, it is called, apparently – and I was exhorted to take with it the most grotesque pickled gherkin. The nice man behind the counter wouldn't accept a penny payment for my food nor the several strong cups of coffee I drank. It was on the house, he said, proffering me a huge slice of something oddly called cheesecake. I was just the latest in a line of celebrities who had patronized his 'Deli' and he knew that I had been flung ashore with neither money nor belongings to my name. A little food and coffee was the least he could offer me.

Well, I was mortified, Nellie. Accepting charity like that! I also felt rather full, as I thanked him, shame-faced. But, I thought, beggars can't be choosers. I asked him where I might find a ladies' costumiers of some kind – not too expensive – and he sent me off in the direction of Bloomingdale's, further down Broadway, which was apparently the long, colourful, rather rowdy street I had wandered onto. I walked in a slightly overfed daze down that boulevard of flashing lights and lurid hoardings, marvelling all the while. Here I was – on Broadway! It felt almost hollow and unreal, experiencing it all, and the push and crush of the crowd, by myself. What was I thinking of – coming here alone?

It was in my mind that I would buy a demure and inexpensive outfit and attend the first of these soirees I had been invited to, this very evening. In Bloomingdale's I was told my money was no good (which was just as well!) and the peach and champagne evening frock I picked out was simply handed to me, gratis, by the management. I donned it at once, in their changing rooms, and swallowed my qualms. I looked rather lovely, even though I do say so myself.

Then, I asked the doorman to hail me a cab (really, listen to me, Nellie! Do I not sound like a native New Yorker?) and, once inside, I asked the cabman to direct his horses to the address on the party invitation. A certain function room at the Plaza hotel, back near the park. Well, I rode in style, and the evening was balmy and I grew rather warm at the thought of being in company again. I checked the invitation once more. Yes, it was real. These people – society folk – wanted to see me!

I tottered into the sumptuous foyer of the Plaza hotel. I rode up in an elevator and took directions from the man who pressed the buttons. Then I found myself entering a gilded ballroom, fragrant with lilies, murmurous with genteel conversation. I handed over my invitation, took the glass of champagne they offered me, and prepared to step into the fray.

But guess whose face was the first I saw, Nellie?

Guess whose booming voice was the first to greet me?

I couldn't believe it. He was beaming at me through that foolish beard of his. Professor Zarathustra.

'Mrs Danby!' he cried. 'How delightful to see you again!'

TWELVE
MRS DANBY

My Dearest Nellie,

'What are *you* doing here?!'

I couldn't help shouting. In truth, my voice went a bit screechy at the sight of him, and a few heads turned in our direction. A few disdainful expressions looked our way, but then they saw we were the English guests and our expostulations were evidently put down to eccentricity, or some such. Meanwhile I was glaring hatefully at the bulky and bearded professor. I had hoped never to clap eyes on the brute again. Oh, he was the picture of smugness, Nellie. A gargantuan dandy in a black silk tie and evening dress.

'I thought you'd been arrested at the dock! Didn't they come for you? Didn't we see you dragged away, kicking and shouting? Didn't they lock you up for holding us at gunpoint and kidnapping us and taking us to the bottom of the sea?'

He simply laughed at my noisy indignation. 'I am here because I was invited, my dear Mrs Danby. For more or less the same reason as yourself, I imagine.' He grinned and took my hand to kiss it. I felt that black beard bristle on my skin again and I almost dropped my glass of champagne. 'I am the toast of the town, my dear. They couldn't keep me locked up for long, now, could they? Professor Zarathustra is a hero! Everyone wants to know more about his terrifying escapade under the waves.'

'Pah,' I snorted. I really did snort. I was rather proud of how outraged I could sound. I tried to push past him, keen to meet my high society hostess, but Zarathustra dogged me through the crowd. There was a dance band playing light, jaunty, modern tunes and how I longed to be away from him. I wanted to forget all about those nasty goings-on at sea.

'I think I have found the way, Mrs Danby,' the Professor said, grasping hold of my arm and swinging me gently about to face him.

'Let me go at once!' I demanded. But I knew what he was like with a fixed idea in his mind. He would tell me his news whether I wanted to hear it or not. I glanced downwards to check that he wasn't about to pull a weapon on me again.

He had a feverish light in his eye and he kept repeating that he had 'found the way.'

'Didn't you read my interview in *The Times*?' I shot back at him. 'Didn't you read that I never want to see you again? I almost died several times, and it was all because of you.'

'Poppycock!' he roared, and everyone looked at us again. People were whispering behind their hands. Our reunion wasn't going unnoticed. 'I saved your life several times, you silly woman. And don't tell me that you weren't excited by the whole thing! Don't tell me that it wasn't the most thrilling thing ever to happen to you!'

I seethed at this. 'I don't want excitement!'

He assured me – very loudly – that I did. Suddenly I saw that the only way of keeping him quiet was to take him aside and pretend to listen to whatever nonsense he had to tell me.

I found a vestibule, where we could sit to one side, away from eavesdroppers. 'Go on, then,' I said wearily. Really, he is the most exhausting man, Nellie. Just being in his presence is enough to sap me dry.

'Magic, Mrs Danby,' he said. 'Did I not say that I would find some means to get us back to that secret undersea city? Fair means or foul? Or, if need be, magical means?'

I looked at him, astonished. 'Magic? You mean, Hey Presto? Abracadabra? Open Sesame?' I tried to laugh this away and he squeezed my arm to shut me up.

He went on then, speaking in a low and urgent voice, to explain how he had contacted some kind of society that was based somewhere he described as 'downtown' in the elegant and leafy Greenwich Village (a place I had already fixed on visiting, as it happens.) Anyhow, this is apparently home to a cabal of magicians and their friends and associates with whom he has involved himself.

I sighed. It sounded as if Zarathustra had embroiled himself with a load of crackpots who, no doubt, were falling over themselves to fawn over him. And, indeed, he revealed that he was staying at the home of the main sorcerer or wizard, or whatever they call themselves. Professor Zarathustra's big news was that, through his new friends, he had heard rumours about a travel agency. A very special kind of travel agency, operating out of somewhere in Lower Manhattan. One that could send its customers on trips to all sorts of improbable places.

He paused and looked at me expectantly.

'And do you believe this?' I asked him.

'Why should they lie to me?' he boomed.

All at once I saw the foolish Zarathustra for just what he was: a credulous child, who would believe in anything anyone tells him. He is, in a way, a kind of innocent. I saw by the fierce light in those eyes that he believed utterly in this chimerical travel agency. Some whispered rumour was enough to send him off rampaging about the place, full of brio and vim. It seemed to me, Nellie, that Zarathustra belonged to a less cynical age than this. And I felt myself sounding very cynical indeed as I laughed in his face.

'A magic travel agency? Oh dear. Oh, you poor man. You silly, deluded fool. I think you must have gone doolally at the bottom of the sea. Starved your brain of oxygen, or something.'

He glared at me hatefully. As if he couldn't believe I could be so cruel. And I was rather thrilled, Nellie, I must admit, at making him so riled. I stood up and told him, 'Now I must greet our host and hostess. Please don't come bothering me again.'

As I moved away – light as a feather in my new, floaty peach dress – I knew that, of course, he would come bothering me again. But perhaps that wouldn't necessarily be a disaster? What do you think, Nellie? Should I have fled at the first sight of that incorrigible man?

In fact, I think I knew really what you would tell me, Nellie. And it's at times like this that I miss having my good sister here with at my side. No doubt you would have counselled me to keep well away from the terrible man. No longer was I being held at gunpoint, aboard a sinking ship, by the man with access to the only means of escape. Here I was in a city of millions, and it should have been quite easy to give that hirsute menace the slip.

But then, I wonder, Nellie. You are rather over-fond, at times, of male company. I do not mean to judge, my dear. I wonder how you would have reacted to the attentions of such an impressive man as Zarathustra? I wonder if his blandishments would have left you chilly? I doubt it, somehow.

However, I moved right away from the babbling, excitable scientist and went to meet my hosts. They were effusive and polite. They were extremely glad to make my acquaintance. A small group of well-dressed party-goers gathered around me to listen to me recount my adventures aboard the *SS Utopia* and under the sea in Professor Zarathustra's miniature vessel. I dislike speaking in public, as you know, dear, and I don't have much time for show-offs. Yet the champagne worked its subtle magic on me and I found myself warming to my theme. I was making hand gestures and raising my voice before I knew it, as I enacted our battle with the giant octopi and our frightening descent into the lowest realms of the deep blue sea. The crowd around me grew larger and still I went on: impersonating the voices and mannerisms of my fellow adventurers.

I wondered at myself, I really did. But how I blushed and basked in the attention when they all applauded the end of my tale. I had just described how the *Asgaard* had sailed into the harbour, where we caught our first glimpse of Lady Liberty... and then I spied Zarathustra's face glowering out of the assembled crowd at me. He looked piqued that I had divulged so many details of our goings-on to our fellow party guests. His face was puce with rage. I saw him turn smartly on his heel and storm out of the Plaza ballroom. I had made a fool of him. And, as far as I was concerned, he thoroughly deserved it.

I hadn't, however, make any mention of his secret underwater city when I had related my tale. I didn't go so far as to reveal all his secrets, so I did have some loyalty after all, though goodness knows why I should. The old fool should have appreciated that. Well, never mind. I never had to clap eyes on him again, did I?

The band started up again and suddenly everyone was dancing. The party had moved on. I was no longer the centre of attention. My hosts and their many guests had finished with me, and were intent on other distractions now.

I hung around for a while, and drifted about the room. All of a sudden, I felt as if I had made myself look rather silly with all my showing off. People smiled and nodded at me, but no one really wanted to talk to me. They had heard enough, perhaps.

I slipped away, out of the party, and headed outside onto the street, passing through that grand foyer once more.

Outside the street was busy. I watched vehicles whizzing by, and recognized, opposite, the entrance to Central Park I had taken last time. I saw signs for the little lake where I had sat, and the zoo. So – I was beginning to get my bearings a little. I even managed to wend my way back to my own hotel, retracing my steps several blocks south.

Perhaps I wouldn't be as keen in future to take up all of those invitations to society do's. Perhaps it would be best if I simply got on with the holiday I had intended to have in the first place? I didn't want to waste my time constantly whooping it up, did I? The evening was starting to feel rather stale to me. I felt somewhat used, like an old dishrag. They had wrung me out and now I was left, limp and alone.

As I passed through the foyer of the Wellington Hotel, the receptionist called to me. Apparently I had another message. This time it was from London, and was marked urgent.

'Oh!' I said, quite pleased, and went to sit on a squashy chair by the fireplace in order to read it. It came from my favourite General Practitioner in all of London.

My pleasure at the sight of his name soon wavered, as I realized that he was in a somewhat stern mood:

"Mrs Danby stop I am terribly concerned stop Your involvement with this Zarathustra person can only lead to disaster stop He is a dangerous madman stop Nightshade Jones also read of adventures in paper and is of same mind stop He has been in touch over same matter stop We are both delighted you survived disaster at sea but lament fact that Zarathustra was involved stop If he contacts you again keep out of his way stop. Repeat: Zarathustra is a lunatic stop,

Yours, John Wilson MD stop."

Well, that's Mr Wilson for you, Nellie. He always was, in my experience, a bit of a worrywart. Often he hung back when what was really needed was swift, decisive action. However, in this case, I decided that he and my erstwhile employer were quite correct. And that evening's encounter at the Plaza hotel had reinforced that feeling. Zarathustra was best avoided. Magical travel agencies indeed! Sorcerers in Greenwich Village..!

So – nipping back to tell my nice young friend at reception (Billy, his name is) that my important telegram came from none other than Dr Wilson and Mr

Jones themselves (he was thrilled!) I retired to my room on the seventeenth floor.

Again I tried to note down my thoughts and observations from my adventures at sea. My foolish new frock was hanging up in the wardrobe and I sat up in bed. The following day I would accept whatever help our embassy could offer, and make a start in earnest on my holiday plans. I would spend my time peacefully and productively, quietly inspecting the museums and the tourist sites, and perhaps, if the weather was good, taking tea in the outdoor café in the park.

I WAS WRITING OUT A PICTURE POSTCARD FROM CENTRAL PARK. ON THE REVERSE was pictured the very café where I was sitting at that very moment with a pot of tea and a bun, enjoying the morning sunshine. The past few days had been very quiet. I had received some money on loan from our embassy, so that was good. I was to expect compensation from the shipping company, apparently! I had seen no more of Zarathustra, which was also good.

Though, that morning, strolling in the park, I couldn't quite shake the suspicion that someone was following me. I even mentioned it in the postcard I was writing to you, Nellie – but then decided I shouldn't send it, for fear of alarming you. I was most probably imagining it.

But there was a rustling in the bushes, you see. As if someone was keeping pace with me. But I decided that it was nothing. When I looked there was no one there. And besides it was the middle of the day and I was sitting in the open air. There were people about.

But Nellie! All of a sudden there was a hand on my shoulder!

A very cold hand!

THIRTEEN
VAN HALFLING

from the journal of doctor abraham van halfling

THIS MORNING IN THE PARK MRS DANBY WAS DELIGHTED TO SEE ME. WHEN I approached her at her table in the outdoor café, her face lit up at the very sight of me. She seemed to jump up in her chair and give an involuntary shiver. Dare I even hope that this remarkable woman reciprocates the strong feelings I have for her?

When I sat down opposite her, she simply stared, open-mouthed and agog. She stammered out a greeting, and collected together the various writing implements and cards she had scattered across the table.

Politely I enquired how she was finding her stay in New York. Several days had elapsed since our arrival at the docks, and I trusted that she had found adequate means to entertain herself. I told her that I hoped that she had been having a pleasant time. A busy time, at any rate, I imagined, following the publicity she had received in the press on her arrival. Ach, certainly she had been too busy to contact me at my nearby hotel, the Algonquin, in order to keep our dinner appointment which we had discussed aboard the damaged submersible when our lives were in utmost peril and death seemed an inevitability.

But, never mind. The lady assured me that she had been having a very sociable time of it. In fact, I believe she even referred to it as a 'social whirl.' She had attended some kind of ball at the Plaza Hotel, even. I nodded and smiled, pretending to be impressed, and sharing her pleasure in such superficial fripperies. I, too, was invited to many parties and soirees and functions upon arrival in New York, but I turned them all down, curtly and irrevocably. They could not own me. Not for the price of a few drinks and some foolish canapés. Van Halfling would be no hostess's novelty guest, no matter how lofty her position in society.

I explained all of this to Mrs Martha Danby as we sat in the sunshine, and I clicked my fingers for a glass of iced tea. The waiter took his time about bringing it, but this merely afforded me more moments to observe Mrs Danby as she drank her own. I told her how much I admired her new outfit, which seemed to my inexpert eye very modish. We shared rueful stories about having to dash out and acquire new travelling wardrobes, having lost most everything but what we stood up in to the sinking of the *Utopia*.

'Alack, many of my notes and papers went to the bottom of the sea, also,' I sighed. 'Ach. Here was I, alive and saved and all, but a speechifier without speeches. A lecturer without lectures.'

'Goodness!' gasped Mrs Danby. And I remembered how, just as all the signs were indicating that we were going to have to abandon ship, she had returned to her cabin and rescued her own papers. 'Well, what can you do?' she asked. 'You have all of these speaking engagements coming up, all across the country.'

I nodded and sighed. 'Ach, I have had to devote most of the hours of the past few nights and days to the rewriting and the reconstructing of my lectures. I have had to relive and reword everything I ever wrote. A gargantuan task! But it is over. And I think my lectures are probably even better than they previously were.'

'Oh!' said Mrs Danby, with that charming quirk to her eyebrows as she smiled at me. 'Every cloud, eh?'

'What?' I asked her.

'A silver lining,' she added.

'Ach, yes,' I said, though I do not believe there is any truth in that cliché whatsoever. Van Halfling knows that there can be many, many dark clouds and not a silver lining to be seen for anything. Clouds dark as hell with no silvery bits at all. That is what Van Halfling knows. But let Mrs Danby live in her bright, optimistic world. Why spoil it for her? I decided to ask her out to dinner again.

'Yes, yes, of course,' she said. She was staring into my face with concern. 'Why are you so pale and drawn?' she asked. 'Is it just because you have spent your days and nights rewriting? Or is it... something else?'

That clever, sensitive woman's intuition! Ach, she is a marvel. Somehow she could see it plainly upon my face that I had been through an extraordinary adventure.

'There is... something else,' I confided in her.

She ordered some fiendishly sugary donuts for us. She said I looked as if I hadn't eaten for days. This was quite true, as it happens.

And so I ate donuts and related to her some of the events of the past few days. It all came about because of my rewriting of my lectures. One day, I had been locked inside my room, scratching away, and I realized I needed some air before I went insane. To that end I walked downtown, several dozen blocks down the island. I was heading vaguely towards the university and Greenwich Village, thinking I could find a tearoom and perhaps continue with my writing there, in more convivial surroundings.

And there, while I was stalking around those quaint, twisting, leafy streets in Greenwich, I bumped into our mutual acquaintance.

'Not Professor George Edward Zarathustra!' Mrs Danby let out a groan.

'Ach, the very one,' I told her. And then I told her how, even though I tried to wriggle from the mad fellow's grasp, he wouldn't let go, but thrust that unfortunate beard right into my face and insisted loudly that I come with him to some kind of meeting.

'Oho!' said Mrs Danby at this, as if she knew exactly what kind of meeting it would be.

I told her: it was a meeting of sorcerers, wizards and necromancers. The cream of New York's underground magicians and witches were gathering together that night for one of their regular 'shindigs', as Zarathustra put it. He was twisting my arm, telling me I would find it all fascinating. He had already been to a meeting or two and was well in with the whole shady lot of them. Well, I could feel myself weakening. I could sense my own fascination with the arcane rising up in me, and so I relented! I foolishly let myself be swept along by Zarathustra – even though I knew, with that devil involved, the whole thing would turn out to be a disaster.

And I wasn't wrong.

The meeting that night was in a very decrepit corner of the old town of Greenwich. Somewhere between the harbour and a row of coffee shops. A tall old townhouse was lit up with lanterns and fairy lights and some strange kind of music was issuing out of its open front door. A dank, yellowish mist was descending as Zarathustra and I hurried up the garden path into the home of Henry Grenoble. Arch mage and collector of arcane books. He was a shortish, bald, effusive man, who welcomed us in his hallway. He was like a genial pixie, with tufted eyebrows and a pointed nose. You could see how he could be easily roused to temper, though, by his darting, suspicious eyes, which gave the lie to his smiles.

He seemed delighted to see Zarathustra again. And when Zarathustra introduced me, he almost fell over. 'Van Halfling! Here! In my humble abode!'

Luckily, I had a number of choice stakes slid into the lining of my cape –

which I refused to let the servants take from me. Just in case – at this unholy soirée – I met with any of the undead. Which seemed only too likely, I thought. Zarathustra led me about the place, behaving as if he had known this place for years. He introduced me to a plethora of bizarre-looking people. 'Didn't I tell you?' he asked. 'This is where I'm staying. Henry Grenoble has been kind enough to offer me a wing of this house, for as long as I care to stay.'

'Huh,' said Mrs Danby, sitting opposite me in the park. 'That Zarathustra always lands on his feet, doesn't he?'

'Ach, indeed,' I said. 'And he behaved that evening as if the whole elegant house belonged to him.'

Mrs Danby tutted at this, but I could tell that she wanted to hear more. Somehow she was still intrigued by that bearded reprobate and his doings.

I told her of the queer people I met that night: practitioners of many kinds of unspeakable arts. I examined the old books on the shelves and several alarming paintings and *objets d'art*. I enquired – quite casually – about the extent of the vampire contagion on the eastern seaboard, and got ribald laughter in reply. I was forced to drink a most potent cocktail, which was purple and steaming.

Just when I thought I had eluded him in the exotic melee, Zarathustra dragged me aside, into an antechamber. Then he started talking at me in a low, urgent voice. I waved him away, feebly, but then, as he talked, I found that I must listen. As you know, I have an endless fascination for the arcane and the magical, and it has – alack – led me up a few hazardous garden paths.

'What do you mean?' Mrs Danby asked me, finishing up the last of the donuts fastidiously. She had a fine moustache of sugary frosting as she leaned forward to quiz me.

'He started telling me about a particular travel agency, with an office somewhere close to Grenoble's townhouse.'

'A travel agency?' Mrs Danby echoed, looking quite unsurprised.

'Yes, Zarathustra said it was just the ticket. It is owned by a very special person, who will be able to grant the Professor the thing he most desires.'

Mrs Danby rolled her eyes. 'That thing being a return trip to his precious undersea kingdom.'

She sounded so dismissive, even I felt defensive on the Professor's behalf. 'But we saw it too, Mrs Danby. We saw that gleaming city, didn't we? And we owe it to the world to learn more.'

'We saw something,' she conceded. 'But frankly, I don't see what the fuss is about learning more about it. Why does the world care? And what would the world do, even if it knew about this place? Offer weekend breaks there? Holidays of a lifetime?'

Mrs Danby was squawking now, enjoying her own silly jokes. Perhaps she is not the woman I imagined. Perhaps she lacks the sort of depth and sensitivity that I fondly imagined?

Professor Zarathustra had no qualms about using my fondness for the Danby of my imaginings. He said, 'Think how Mrs Danby would be impressed. Just think of the tale you could tell her, Van Halfling, if you came with me tonight, in order to investigate...'

Me? Why did the great Professor Zarathustra need Van Halfling's help? I put this to him, incredulously. Surely he never needed anyone's assistance?

At this he became rather endearingly gruff and shy. 'Well, the thing is, you see,' he said, lowering his voice. 'I tend to bluster, rather, Van Halfling, old man. I hear that the one who runs this travel agency place is a subtle and conniving old cove. More than one of my new friends has told me to tread carefully. And I know how you are so accustomed to working with slippery and nefarious types...'

Ach, and so he got me by flattery, and also by hinting that Mrs Danby might be impressed by the two of us having further adventures together, which I might soon relate to her, sitting in the sun, taking tea in the park. Just as I was doing now, in fact, although, to be honest, Mrs Martha Danby was looking distinctly unimpressed with my narrative.

'So you went with him? To this place?' She gripped the café table and leaned forward urgently. 'After everything we went through? At the bottom of the ocean? When we nearly died? You still went with him?'

'Indeed I did,' I said firmly. 'And, as a result, I had one of the most bizarre experiences of my life.'

'It serves you right,' she snapped. There was a pause and she added, 'Well, go on then! Don't leave me dangling!'

And so I told her, how Zarathustra and I slipped out of the party in that Greenwich Village townhouse just before midnight. We hurried through the winding streets, past dimly lit shop fronts, and then across Washington Square, which showed few signs of life that late night. Soon we were in what Zarathustra called the East Village, and he seemed to know exactly where he was going. Here we slipped away from the bright street lights and into a warren of stinking alleyways. A network of fire escapes was etched against the starless skies. We hurried so deeply into this urban labyrinth that I should never have been able to find my way out again, alone.

At length we came to the back of an old warehouse, and Zarathustra bade me to clamber up a clanging, rusty fire escape, up to the fourth floor. Here there was a door covered in flaky pink paint and the poorly painted legend, 'The World of Mumu'.

Zarathustra grinned at me and knocked sharply on the door.

It squeaked open, revealing blackness within.

'Come on then,' urged my companion. 'Get in!'

I took a deep breath and stepped into the darkness.

It was as if we were stepping into someone's terrible clutches. I felt it at once. Zarathustra was foolhardy, and we had blundered into a trap.

Then: 'Welcome!' said a voice in the darkness. It was the most ghastly voice I had ever heard in my life.

And that's saying something. I am Doctor Abraham Van Halfling, you know!

FOURTEEN
MRS DANBY

My Dearest Nellie,

I didn't send you the postcard I was writing when Van Halfling jumped out of the bushes at me. Much too alarming and melodramatic.

But there I was, at the café in Central Park, minding my own beeswax and having a lovely time with an iced bun and a pot of tea, when the cold hand touched my shoulder. Then I was renewing my acquaintance with that dapper fiend-slayer, Abraham Van Halfling, who sat down with me in the sunshine and proceeded to regale me with tales of his adventures since we said our farewells at the docks in Lower Manhattan.

Quite honestly, Nellie, I was not sure whether the man was mad or daft. His tales were certainly outlandish. You really haven't heard anything yet.

Nevertheless, I agreed to go out to dinner with him that evening. We were to dine at his hotel, the Algonquin, not far from my own. Perhaps I was mad, too, for electing to spend more time with that fascinating man. Do you think? I confess I was delighted and intrigued to see him again in the park. Even if what he told me was gallingly ridiculous.

Van Halfling promised that he would tell me more that evening, as we enjoyed dinner at the Algonquin. Quail eggs and lobster tails, he promised. I was thrilled at the prospect of donning my new glad rags to meet him. I sprayed myself with a delicious new scent – rather like jasmine. And I anticipated an evening hearing all about these two friends of mine and how they fell into the clutches of an insidious Chinaman called Mumu.

THE DINING ROOM WAS A PICTURE. SO SOPHISTICATED. ALL THE LUXURIES YOU could imagine. A man was playing show tunes on a piano as we sat at our table, in the far corner. The cutlery and crockery were of such delightful quality. I couldn't help myself smoothing the pristine tablecloth and napkins as Van Halfling talked. Abraham. He asked me to call him Abraham, and now, at last, that gallant gent was learning to call me Martha.

We had dainty and fancy food. The likes of which I myself had prepared back in London, and had the pickings of afterwards with the rest of the staff when I was in service. But no one had ever presented me with such a banquet of heavenly foodstuffs before. I felt treated like a queen.

But still, even this opulence of the setting and the lavishness of the fare was as nothing but a backdrop to what Abraham was telling me. Even several hours later, sitting up in bed and reliving the evening, I couldn't quite believe what he had told me. But I had to believe! Why would he lie to me?

I relate the details here for you, my dear sister.

As promised, they were offered the chance of visiting anywhere they so desired. The Chinaman stood behind a plain, empty desk and bowed with mock supplication. Abraham said that they felt he was secretly mocking him. There was a sly, underhand irony about every word that he uttered.

Zarathustra was sweating. He was damply over-excited, apparently. He burst forth in stentorian tones, as usual, playing his full hand and declaring his heart's desire. 'I want to go to the secret undersea city!' he cried, with no more guile than a child of six, Abraham said. Yet I could tell that Van Halfling harbours a sneaking liking for the Professor.

But this ardent request was brutally put down by the Chinaman, Mumu, who sneered. He told Zarathustra, 'You are too desperate. You must learn patience. This... this is delicate magic. Very delicate and sensitive. Your heart is pounding. Your blood is thundering through the vessels and chambers of your body. Sending you to your heart's desire in this condition would upset the balances.'

Zarathustra looked piqued at this, says Abraham. His great black beard bristled and he fumed. 'What?!'

But the Chinaman was calm. He turned to Van Halfling. 'You. You are not like your companion. It is given to you to choose your first destination. Your impossible first destination.'

Abraham had to spend some moments calming Zarathustra down. The Professor ranted and raved for a while. Why should Van Halfling go first? Who cared about where he wanted to go? Zarathustra didn't want to go anywhere Abraham would choose. Then he started demanding that Van Halfling use his turn to choose the undersea city for himself.

'No,' the Chinaman interrupted them. 'It must be his own free choice.'

I must say, Nellie, by this point I was agog. I hadn't noticed our soup bowls being removed and dainty little plates of salad and pale green boiled eggs placed before us in their stead. I was hooked on Abraham's words. He was quite the raconteur. 'So you chose a destination?' I asked. 'You plucked one out of the air?'

'Ach yes,' said Abraham, picking up a quail's egg and peeling it very deliberately. 'I chose somewhere truly incredible and impossible. With the avowed aim of proving this Mumu person a charlatan.'

'And?' said I. 'Where did you choose?'

'I whimsically chose the planet Mars. I chose as our destination the canals of the planet Mars.'

He popped the whole egg into his mouth as I stared at him.

'What?!'

'And do you know what? That Chinaman didn't turn a hair. Ach, he simply pressed his fingers together in a supplicatory gesture and bowed to us both. And then he turned and bade us follow him into a corridor that was full of differently coloured doors...'

⁂

THAT NIGHT I HAD REMARKABLY LURID AND GARISH DREAMS.

Perhaps it was the rich food I ate at the Algonquin, or the extra glass of champagne that Abraham pressed upon me and insisted I take. Maybe it was even the excitement of having all that male attention to myself, and being treated to such a night on the town. It could well be all of these remarkable things, but I suspect it was mostly down to the story I had been told.

I lay in my sumptuous bed and dreamed of corridors filled with doors. Differently sized and differently coloured doors, each with all kinds of knobs on. They each led to separate destinations. Somehow, magically, they would transport the unwary traveller to impossible places. An insinuating, giggling travel agent was my guide as I crept down that dark corridor. Nellie, I had the heebie-jeebies all night.

I have no doubt that Abraham's words had been so vivid over our supper that I was seeing things quite as they had been for both him and Professor Zarathustra. I experienced both their excitement and dread as they were drawn into the inescapable depths of the World of Mumu.

The travel agent led them to one particular door, painted a brilliant scarlet.

'Here. This door,' he said, 'will lead you to where you want to go. Do not worry about breathing. The atmosphere is fine. Everything is perfect for you.' Then he went on to explain to them quite how expensive this trip was going to be, a fact which Van Halfling waved away, as if it were of no import. I began to suspect, Nellie, that my dining companion was rather well-to-do.

'Beyond that door...' thundered Zarathustra quizzically, 'lies the means for our journeying to the planet Mars?'

The Chinaman merely bowed his head, giggling softly. 'I give you twenty-four hours in the realm that you, Abraham Van Halfling, have chosen of your own free will. In fully one day's time, I will open this door again. But I will not open it for long. You must be ready and waiting for me on the other side, otherwise you will be stuck there for ever.'

Van Halfling said that he nodded quickly, and eagerly. 'Ach, we understand, err, Mumu.'

Then Abraham embarked on the most outrageous and quite simply the pottiest part of his narrative so far, Nellie, as he reached the point when the Chinaman opened to door to reveal...

Not the means for travelling there, but... the Red Planet itself!

The door swung open smoothly onto a dazzling, scarlet desert, with a pinkish sky and burnished golden clouds. A delightfully hot breeze wafted out to the two entranced gentlemen, and the Chinese urged them to step through the threshold to meet it. 'I give you Mars,' he told them.

Well, Nellie, Abraham's voice was very steady and earnest as he told of how he and Zarathustra stepped through that door, onto the crimson sands of the Martian desert. It wasn't unpleasantly hot. It was delightful, he said. A dry heat, that buoyed them up, and made them feel lighter in their ageing forms. Something to do with gravity, I believe, and it had them hopping and bouncing across the dunes. They cried out in glee and laughed out loud, he said, in sheer excitement. They had stepped out of that dingy corridor in that obscure warehouse and been instantaneously whisked onto the shimmering surface of an exotic and impossibly distant world.

Van Halfling looked backwards, to see the red-painted door standing open some way behind them. It stood by itself, incongruously. Darkness beyond its frame, and the Chinaman bidding them a silent, sly adieu. Abraham said he almost cried out as the door slammed shut and swiftly disappeared, but he reigned in his feelings of panic.

'We are alone on the Red Planet,' he told himself. 'Miraculously – we are here. And we must make the most of it. We have twenty-four hours.' He looked to where Zarathustra had drifted and bounced – he was in the next sandy gully, and Abraham realized that he must take careful stock of where the door had been and where it would be again in a day's time. But did that mean an Earth day? Or a Martian day? And what was the difference?

My head was spinning at the thought of such things, Nellie, and I think Van Halfling's did, too. But Zarathustra would know. He was a scientist, was he not? With such knowledge at his fingertips.

Abraham was feeling very out of his depth. And so was I, Nellie, hearing all of this.

He told me that they had an astonishing time on that far distant planet. Zarathustra came out of his sulk and howled with triumphant mirth at being the first Englishman on Mars. Van Halfling, it turns out, is Dutch (which I never knew! His accent is so gentlemanly!) He was very struck then, to see the canals of Mars, so similar to those of his native Holland.

The next day I met Van Halfling to spend the day with him, and to hear more details about his adventures.

I found that I was ever so keen to hear the rest of his adventures.

But... was he mad, Nellie? Or was I? Only a week before I would have dismissed his words as the ravings of a madman. Or I would have suspected that the Chinaman had drugged him somehow, with the smoke from that foul poppy they're all so keen on. And perhaps that was still the truth of it. Either way – whether he went to Mars or not – Abraham Van Halfling had done something unique in my experience, Nellie.

He had – I hardly dared think it or write it down in a letter to you, my dear sister – but he had succeeded in catching my fancy...!

from the journal of doctor abraham van halfling

ACH, WHAT AN AMAZING WOMAN. MRS MARTHA DANBY IS EVERYTHING I could ever wish to find in a woman. She has, as I have already learned, great fortitude and courage and, when the chips are down, she has moral fibre the equal of anyone. These past few days in New York I have discovered another side to her. The patient, listening, unjudging portion of her being. It has been I – Abraham Van Halfling – to whom she has sat and listened with such patience and intelligence, as I burbled out the tale of my recent adventures. As we sat at dinner, or in the park, or strolled the endless canyons of the city's avenues, she never once interrupted me, stopped me, or declared me mad.

How many women would take it on trust that their male companion was speaking the truth when he told her had visited the planet Mars?

I can only put it down to the fact that, as the ex-housekeeper of the very excellent Mr Nightshade Jones of Balcombe Street, Mrs Danby is quite used to hearing the most outlandish things from the lips of gentlemen of her acquaintance.

Martha. That dear lady has exhorted me to call her Martha.

She has a most kindly visage, and a well-upholstered body that is pleasingly puddingy and, I imagine, most pleasant in every regard. I hardly understand the words I am writing. I am trying to give an account of my adventures of late, but my thoughts keep returning to this lady. And this is I – Van Halfling – who swore off feeling affection for any of the fairer sex. As would any demon hunter who had encountered as many succubae, incubi and variously naughty ladies as I have in my time. But there is something rather remarkable about Martha Danby. Her eyes twinkle at me and – ahh – there is a scent of garlic, or perhaps jasmine about her.

Ach, but she must, deep down, think I am a babbling fool. Or one who is trying too hard to impress her. Far too hard, with his wild claims to have journeyed in one night to the surface of the planet Mars. Along with our mutual acquaintance – Professor George Edward Zarathustra – I have recently returned from a twenty-four hour impossible sojourn to the Red Planet. I know that I speak the truth, and yet I also know how ludicrous it sounds.

I watched Zarathustra's grumpy ire turn swiftly into boyish delight. He skipped and bounced across the dunes and together we explored the deeply rutted, dried-up canals and tried to picture what kinds of vessels once sailed upon them. We stared in speechless delight at the bright spectacle of our own world in the sky as it rose beyond all those pink and golden banks of cloud.

We were both relieved to find the atmosphere breathable, despite all the received wisdom we'd heard that stated the contrary. In fact, it was rather delicious, tasting somewhat of Turkish Delight, I thought. The gravity was doing something strange, too, allowing us to prance and soar through the air like members of some bally Russian ballet. I'm afraid to say that –far from being at all scientific about our trip – we disported ourselves for quite some time, disgracefully – hopping about and even turning cartwheels. All of this was great fun until we saw the living Martians.

Mrs Danby – Martha – was particularly surprised and alarmed to hear this part of my narrative. We were walking through the zoo in Central Park as I explained to her the kinds of Martians we had encountered. First of all there were the tall, skinny green ones with two sets of arms and more or less human faces. They wore loin clothes, carried club-like weapons and seemed to represent the underclass. We first espied them as they worked in one of the canals, seemingly using brush pans and shovels to collect glittering dust and pop it into sacks.

Then as we explored further, we came to a ruined city, where the remains of dwellings were formed of some strange, rubberlike material. Here we felt the presence of ghostly beings, who trailed tendrils, like jellyfish do, as they haunted their once-great conurbation. Zarathustra and I hid in the ancient rubble as we watched them passing to and fro. We saw them whirl about in a stately dance of their own, until they were scattered by the coming of tall, multi-limbed metal creatures that stalked through the valley, blasting at things with sizzling heat rays, seemingly for the fun of it.

Zarathustra looked most perplexed by all of this life on Mars.

Luckily, he managed to keep quiet and not cry out too much. Even when the silvery, priest-like beings with cat-eyes emerged from one of the more solid buildings and engaged in a telepathic duel of some kind with the warlike metal giants. It was all quite a spectacle, I must say, and I don't imagine that humble Earthlings such as I understood much of it. We saw the tripod creatures retreat, and the cat-eyed priests in their silver capes stood there looking pleased with themselves. At this point I could sense Professor Zarathustra's urgent need to burst out of our cover and into the open. 'I must go to them Van Halfling! Imagine! The first contact between human and alien! It has to be Zarathustra! Surely the honour belongs to the greatest hero-scientist of our age? George

Edward Zarathustra!'

Of course, by now, he was up on his feet and shouting boastfully. There was nothing I could do to stop the fool. And, no sooner was he bellowing and strutting about, than those silvery-caped priest-like beings shot across the waste ground and were staring at us both in something that I can only describe as horror.

And that was how we found ourselves in the alien zoo. We were rendered unconscious by some dashed futuristic device and woke up goodness knows how much later to find ourselves in a metal cell with a fourth wall of sizzling energy, facing a whole lot of other creatures of the most extraordinary types, in cells of their own. I looked at Zarathustra and was absolutely livid with him for showing off. We didn't even know how much time had passed. There was no way of telling. Plus, we didn't know how far we were from where the Chinaman would make the magic door rematerialize. In short, we were a hopeless case. And we had been made to wear horrible rags, as well.

The Martians came to look at us with their catlike eyes. They poked and prodded us and this made Zarathustra roar like a bear. He was even angrier than I was. Ach, I felt very naked and defenceless without my coat stuffed with wooden stakes and knives.

Martha Danby was starting to look rather alarmed by this point in my recitative. 'I would just have died,' she said. 'Really! I wouldn't have known what to do! I would have given up!'

We were feeding the sea lions in the Central Park zoo, tossing them bits of fish heads and guts, which the keeper had kindly lent us. The foolish bobbing and snapping of the aquatic animals seemed so benign next to some of the alien horrors I had encountered of late.

'So what did you do?' Martha asked at last, gazing into my abstract expression.

'Ach,' I sighed, shivering in the spring air. Was it only a matter of days since I had fled across those burning sands with Zarathustra in our rags? With hordes of furious Martians at our heels? 'Well,' I said. 'Zarathustra came into his own. His dander was up. He challenged the leader of the Martians to a duel. He smashed up our cell, made an awful hullaballoo and demanded that the Martian High Priest meet him in mortal combat in their sacred arena. And so, to my mortification and shame, the next thing I'm witnessing is this terrible fight – with both Zarathustra and the man he's challenged riding about on the backs of purple lizard-tiger things, slashing at each other with spears and daggers. Anyhow, Zarathustra's pretty good in a fight of any kind, it seemed, and victory was his. Though, it turns out, Martians aren't terribly honourable and don't keep their word, and so as a consequence we had to fight our way out of the horrible city and run all the way back to the desert. With hordes of the things at our backs. Screaming blue murder.'

'Goodness,' said Martha, handing back the gory bucket to the zoo keeper, and looking queasy. Though whether this was to do with the fish guts or my account of our adventure, I don't really know. We turned away from the barking sea lions, and I slid my arm through her own and we walked like that, linked together, towards the hooting monkey house. 'Oh, yes, indeed. By some miraculous chance, we had timed it to perfection. Bloody, bruised, battered and covered in rags, Zarathustra and I burst over the final crimson dune and there – wonder of wonders – was the open portal. And, standing inside its frame, was the curiously welcoming sight of the Chinese travel agent. He seemed not one whit alarmed by our desperate states. He took not the slightest notice of the army of Martians at our backs. He simply held open the door for us as we hurtled through. And then he stepped through after us, and pulled it firmly shut.

'Zarathustra and I stood panting in the dark corridor. It was cold now, with the hot breath of Mars stopped up behind that door.

'It took us a long time to catch our breath. We simply stared at each other and Mumu, who steepled his fingers and smiled at us. Inscrutably.

'"I shall make up your bill,' he said, and turned to lead us back to his shabby office.

'Ach, I had left my finest cloak on Mars. Lined with shot red silk, with pockets for all my weapons and assorted demon-related paraphernalia. But, as Zarathustra pointed out, as we hurried out of there, and down the twisting fire escape: we were lucky to still have our lives. He sounded shaken and disturbed. Even more than during our adventure at sea. But I must admit, he had displayed astonishing courage in facing and dispatching that Martian high priest in a duel. As we said our goodbyes on the fringes of Chinatown – preparing to go our separate ways in the night-time gloom – I clapped Zarathustra heartily on the back. Excellent fellow! Our trip to Mars has quite altered my perception of him as an addle-pated idiot. He is still an over-educated buffoon – but he has the strength and bravery of a lion, to boot.'

Mrs Martha Danby waited until my story had quite ended until she asked me a question she had obviously been wrestling with. We were looking at the parakeets in their elaborate cages, and I was wondering whether we ought to find somewhere to eat. She turned to me and said, 'But, Abraham, are you sure, now? Can it really be? This man Mumu... might he perhaps have drugged you somehow? Fed you some noxious kind of potion? Could you smell anything strange? Did he hypnotise you? Did he do anything unusual to make you think you had travelled so easily to another world?'

My heart sank a little. So she didn't believe me after all. She must have seen the disappointment in my face because she burst out, over the noise of the squawking birds, 'Oh, don't believe that I doubt a word of your account! Please don't think that. I am simply overwhelmed by it, and by the vividness of your memories and the eloquence of your telling. My mind is trying hard to cope with the bizarreness of it all...'

Excellent woman! She was trying hard to believe me.

I put my arm around her and we walked out of the zoo, and to the edge of the park, where I flagged down a smart coach and pair. I instructed the driver to take us once around the whole park, so that we might enjoy the evening air, and sit in pleasant quiet. Jogging along, under the spread boughs of the trees and the gas lamps as they were lit one after the next, I fancied that I could relax. I could no longer smell that sweetish Martian air or feel its heat upon my skin. I could let the terrors of recent days fall away from me. I could relax and put my arm around Mrs Martha Danby.

That was... until we reached a particularly shady stretch of road, where no one walked and the lamps weren't on yet. Here, our horses gave a whinnying shriek and our cabman cried out in alarm. Martha sat up quickly, 'What is it?' she screeched.

I was on my feet and I already knew. Three figures were standing on the cobbled road in front of our cab, which had been forced to stop quite abruptly. Four more figures emerged from the dark bushes. We were being ambushed by hoodlums. They stepped forward menacingly.

'Robbers!' cried Mrs Martha Danby.

But I had seen the glinting of their fangs in the newly-risen moonlight. These were no ordinary brawlers and muggers who had emerged from the darkness to attack us. These snarling young men were... vampires!

My Dearest Nellie,

Oh my goodness, what a day we had! What did our poor mother used to tell us? 'You play with fire and you get burned.' She used this old saying to warn her daughters off paying heed to the wrong kind of men. Or anything, actually. She instilled in us both a fear of all the world that I'm pleased to say hasn't stuck. However, the men I become involved with would have mother spitting feathers. It seems to me that the kind of men I meet are those irresistibly drawn to darkness, death and disaster.

What is it about me that propels me into the world of these strange men?

It was almost midnight in New York City when I got back to my hotel room after another day with Abraham Van Halfling. Sitting up in bed at the Wellington Hotel, I was still quaking with shock and fear. The receptionist, Billy, noticed this at once when I returned to the hotel from my day out.

It should have been such a lovely and romantic day! We fed the animals in the zoo and we sat by the duck pond with soup and crackers. We went to see a painting exhibit together and we drank hot coffee topped with whipped cream in our favourite café. I had all sorts of lovely feelings stirring within me, as I contemplated Van Halfling's noble features, his luxuriant sideburns and his dapper cravat. However, the man would insist on spoiling the day by telling me the most ridiculous stories about time recently spent in the company of that oafish braggart, Professor Zarathustra.

Now, I know that Zarathustra gets embroiled in escapades that anyone normal would assume to be impossible, and I have even been involved in one of those myself, as you well know, sister. But that day Abraham Van Halfling went too far. We were feeding the sea lions and he was burbling on about some kind of sojourn he and the professor recently went on to the planet Mars and I thought to myself: 'Martha, he is crackers. He's doolally tap. How can he believe a word of what he's telling you? And he's being oh-so earnest about it, too. With that kind of lowered-voice, intent-looking, dark-eyed concentration of the very insane.' Mind you, he was looking dishier than ever, the old gent, so I found myself putting up with it.

Oh, why didn't Doctor Wilson warn me about Van Halfling as he warned me to keep away from Professor Zarathustra? Abraham's crazy brand of danger is more insidious and alluring to me...

So the day went on, with my male companion describing these different kinds of beings he has purportedly met on the planet Mars, and how Zarathustra almost came a cropper in gladiatorial combat in an arena. He painted it all in such bright, lurid word-pictures, that I almost found myself starting to believe in it all. We wandered the labyrinth of neat gardens through the park, peering at statues and well-tended plants and I found myself entertaining the thought that perhaps Van Halfling wasn't mad or pulling my leg. What if such travel – through the magic doors of a travel agency – was indeed possible? And, if that were so, where would I choose to go?

You see how relaxed I was in his company? I wandered dreamily through Central Park. I was even entertaining fantastical hypotheticals, Nellie! And you know that isn't really me.

Then came the terrifying portion of our day spent together. It was dusk, and the gas lamps were flaring into yellow life. Abraham decided that we ought to take a coach and pair around the perimeter of the park and observe the city thus. It was indeed lovely, clip-clopping under the foaming blossom of the trees, and I could even feel his arm creeping closer to my shoulders as we sat back in the open-topped cab. What would I do if he tried to kiss me? Would such a gentleman attempt such a thing in the open air? But this is the New World, I thought, and all sorts of things are possible. Suddenly it didn't seem that a little kiss would be all that improper...

But – alas, Nellie – that was when we were attacked by seven deadly vampires.

They leapt out of the bushes and brought our horses to a screaming standstill. The cabman howled and cowered. Seven very pale young men in quite ordinary clothes came advancing on us. Their leader explained that they had come all the way from New Jersey – wherever that is – simply in order to find Van Halfling and to have it out with him. They had trailed him through the city. Watched his every move. They had waited for this opportunity, when he was defenceless on a lonely street. Now it was time to seize their chance.

Abraham was magnificent then, Nellie. He was up on his feet, unbowed and unafraid of these neighbourhood roughs. They grinned at him in a very nasty way: all of them displaying extremely white and pointed fangs. I gripped my handbag very tightly to me – more vampires! It seemed to me that the undead followed Van Halfling about wherever he went. He would never be without a horde of them coming after him, intent on revenge for what he had done to their kind...

Abraham seemed delighted to see them, almost. There was a decided spring in his step as he hopped out of the cab, produced a handful of newly-sharpened stakes from an inside pocket, and proceeded to do battle with the New Jersey boys.

He was a blur of action as he slipped among them. I could hardly credit it. Sometimes he seems so creaky and old. And yet here he was, like a silver-haired gymnast, with his paisley cravat coming untucked as he slashed his stakes and lashed out with both fists. The seven vampires set about him, street-fighting wildly and in a very ungentlemanly fashion. I cried out encouragement from the cab, and thought wildly for a way in which I might help. But I was out of my depth, Nellie. There was nothing I could do to fight vampires!

But Van Halfling didn't need my help. I stood in shocked silence as the old man dispatched one, two, three, four of them – one after another. They crumbled into showers of nasty grave mould and dust. His pointy stakes flashed out – Poof! Poof! – and his assailants were violently atomised, one after the next.

Then the three remaining were beating a hasty retreat into the dark bushes. 'We'll get you! We'll have our revenge for this!' their leader snarled.

'Really?' asked Van Halfling, mildly, as they hurried away. He smoothed down his silver hair and retied his cravat. And then he smiled reassuringly at me. I was standing there with bits of exploded vampire in my new hairdo and down the front of my jacket and skirt. 'I trust you are unhurt?' Abraham asked me, summoning up every ounce of his olde-worlde charm.

I am afraid I was rather cross with him, Nellie. I demanded that he return me to my hotel at once, and there would be no nightcap for us that night. And no little kiss I had been saving up for the occasion. I was horrified and disappointed, Nellie. I had foolishly imagined the possibility of being romantically attached to this man. But now I could see what his everyday life was like. It was gruesome. I wasn't prepared to stand on the sidelines each day, watching him combat evil forces. And me getting vampire dust in my hair and all across my décolletage.

He instructed the cab driver to take us to the Wellington hotel. When we arrived at the door I said a brusque goodnight and hopped out. He called after me, but I was gone before we could make further plans for seeing each other.

Later on, in my bed, I did wonder whether I hadn't been a little bit rash and cruel.

Ah well, I thought. Never mind. I didn't come abroad looking for romance, did I? Tomorrow I would return to my solitary holiday-making, and thank goodness.

WELL, THAT RESOLUTION LASTED ONLY A COUPLE OF DAYS.

I would have been quite content with my own company. I could have kept myself entertained quite happily in the big city. Why, the very night following that deadly fracas in the park, I went to a Broadway show on my own. I sat through three acts of Madame X at the New Amsterdam Theatre on 42nd Street. I was very high up in the Gods, and the place was thick with smoke. I took some buttered popcorn with me, and from what I understood, the play was rather racy.

Afterwards I walked home up Broadway, past all kinds of insalubrious types, hugger-mugger with the respectable theatre audiences and the steam shooting out of the holes in the road and I suddenly felt terribly lonely. Wasn't that ridiculous, Nellie? When I've always been so self-sufficient and undemanding. I tell you though, I was relieved when I stepped into the gilded foyer of the Wellington and Billy handed me a folded note that he said a handsome old gent had left for me. I knew at once that it must have been Abraham. I fairly snatched that note out of Billy's hand.

"My dear Mrs Danby,

"My first speaking engagement is tomorrow at 2.30pm at the New York Public Library, merely a stone's throw from your hotel. I would be incredibly honoured if you consented to attend? It is entitled 'The Dead Walketh Amongst Us'. I am sure you would find it of great interest.

"Yours truly, Abraham VH."

I'm enclosing the actual note for you here, dear Nellie, so that you can see how ornate his hand is. Very elegant, isn't it? And there's a faint whiff of garlic about the notepaper, isn't there?

Well, of course I determined at once that I was going to go. I slept deeply and with great satisfaction that night, knowing that I was going to see the person I might reasonably imagine one day describing as my 'gentleman friend'.

So that next morning I was up and busy titivating myself for this event at the library. The Wellington has its own hair salon, and so mid-morning found me under the driers, taking a cup of coffee and munching on a number of what they call 'cookies' (which are just untidy-looking biscuits), and chatting away with Renee, who is the resident stylist, and rather brash, if you ask me. With my newly dressed hair rock solid and perfect, I asked for directions to the Public library and Billy organized me, though first he complemented me on my coiffure and outfit. He knew where I was off to – and he wished me the best of luck.

It didn't take me long to find the place. It is a vast building of palest stone, with grand steps and pillars, and giant statues of lions guarding its front portico. It was somewhat intimidating, stepping inside its hallowed halls.

There were intelligent-looking folk milling about, speaking in hushed voices. I found a board that advertised various goings-on, chief among them the afternoon talk to be given by one Doctor Van Halfling, entitled 'The Deaf Walketh Among Us', which was an unfortunate misspelling, I thought, and accounted for some of the startled expressions in the room when, at precisely 2.30 pm my friend Abraham began his erudite address.

There were perhaps a hundred of us there to listen (or to lip-read), and I was pleased for Abraham that he was quite such a success. I sat myself demurely somewhere near the back, and admired the mottled stone of the tall archways and the high windows; the brilliance of the chandeliers and the mellow gleam of the polished wood. Someone kept this place absolutely immaculate, and I was ever so impressed. Indeed, it was a shame that some of the audience members were so shabby in comparison. They rather let the place down!

Abraham shuffled his papers and coughed politely at the lectern. He was wearing the most dashing dark grey suit with a high shirt collar. He welcomed us most graciously to what he described as his 'little talk', and explained how he had been invited to a great number of libraries and campuses to discuss his life's work in slaying the undead monsters that threatened the fabric of the civilized world.

The audience sat forward eagerly as he made his opening remarks, and he then proceeded to describe how he had first, as a boy, realized that the world was not quite as it seemed. And that, hidden lurking in the dark corners, there were monsters that only he could see...

I was entranced, Nellie. Abraham, it turns out, is quite an orator!

And just when we were all completely drawn into his discourse... just when we were all completely and utterly entranced...

There came a terrible shouting from the very back row!

A huge, loud, bellowing voice came echoing through the august chamber.

'Hearsay and poppycock! Trumpery and balderdash!'

There were polite gasps of shock. Who dared to be so rude to such a distinguished guest?

Was it a deaf person, perhaps?

But I knew. I recognized that hectoring voice.

And sure enough, when I turned round to give the heckler a nasty look... who should I see – up on his feet and all purple in the face – but that horrid bully, Professor Zarathustra..!

The ghastly man was making his presence felt again!

And I suddenly knew that no good would come of it.

My Darling Mrs George Edward Zarathustra,

I know, my dear. I promised, I know I did.

Several years ago I made you my solemn promise that no more would I stand up in a public lecture hall in which a man of apparent learning was holding forth, and berate him for his ignorance. I know that you made me promise not for the sake of your own embarrassment and mortification – though you suffered from both as I thundered forth with everyone looking on. I know that you beseeched me to desist in future because of the damage I do myself with such verbal attacks on the ignorant. That harm I do my own reputation and my frazzled nerves is simply not worth the satisfaction of letting these people know what I think of them.

Well, I am afraid I have broken my promise with you, my darling wife! Here, so many thousand miles away from your gently calming and admonishing glance, in the heart of the apparently-civilised New York City, I have been up on my feet again – shouting out during a public lecture. Haranguing the guest speaker! Undermining his argument and booming out foul insults! And worse yet – starting a public fracas and a punch-up in the middle of the New York Public Library.

But is Professor George Edward Zarathustra ashamed of these actions? No, indeed! I would have felt far worse had I sat there like a nincompoop – like the rest of that dunderheaded audience and said nothing. Had I never intervened in Doctor Abraham Van Halfling's interminably dull paper, 'The Dead Walketh Among Us', I would have felt less like myself; less of a Zarathustra and – even – less of a friend to that Van Halfling whose company I have grown to enjoy. I have even come to think of him as a friend – in adversity and adventure.

However, as I yelled out: 'Academic idiot!' and 'Abstract obfuscations!' and 'Intellectual pettifogger!' and 'Where's your empirical evidence? Where's your fieldwork?' I could see that Van Halfling was glaring back at me in a very unfriendly manner indeed. His whole face had gone scarlet. His bald head was shining red through his combed-over silver hair. Veins were standing out in his neck. As his talk progressed he was even starting to look dishevelled and distracted. At one point he stopped to glare at his heckler and shouted: 'Would Professor Zarathustra please have the decency to allow me to continue in peace?'

I believe I heard gasps and murmurs at the sound of my name. See, my dear? My infamy follows me even here. I bellowed back from the front row: 'But where is all your evidence, Van Halfling? Everything you've told us is abstract and dry! Mere theory! What about all your juicy tales of actual vampire slaying, eh? What about all the good stuff?'

He looked most discomfited at this, and I realized that he was not very comfortable describing his actual experiences in that murky world of the living dead. I could hardly believe it! I knew for a fact he had fine tales to tell! Could it be that he was scared of being laughed at and discredited? Did he fear to put his neck on the block? I gasped at his lack of courage. He should be more like Zarathustra!

'You should be more honest and brave!' I cried, on my feet now, with my voice carrying so that the whole room could hear. 'You should tell the good people all about the children of the night whom you have slain with your own hands!'

'Sssh,' said Van Halfling, furiously. I caught a glimpse of that woman – Mrs Danby – seated in the audience and staring furiously at me.

'But it's no secret, is it?' I shouted. 'Doesn't everyone know that you kill monsters for a living, all over the world? That you even reportedly put paid to that famous fiend, Kristoff Alucard..?'

Various other voices were raised now, in competition with my own. Some were telling me to be quiet and desist; others were crying out in response to what I was saying; others, I believe were just shouting out for the sake of it. For the sheer pleasure of lots of lovely noise at a public talk. That's what it needed! It had been too dull and respectable before! There's nothing like a good barney. Yet Van Halfling looked most annoyed.

'But how can you merely orate,' I beseeched him, 'about the dangers of dark forces? How can you merely speculate about the marvels of the mysterious world? You must come clean, sir, and tell us all about how you have actually investigated and encountered them!'

Van Halfling was clambering down from his podium. He had taken off his jacket and was rolling up his immaculate shirtsleeves. The rest of the audience were on their feet and there was a great deal of pushing and shoving going on. It was marvellous, my dear! It was more like being at a boxing match than anything else.

'Tell them the unvarnished truth, Van Halfling! Like Zarathustra does! Embrace the truth of the impossible world! Tell them how we have found a secret city under the water! Tell them how the two of us explored the surface of the Red Planet and met the Martians face to face!'

Van Halfling merely came over to where I was shouting, drew back his fist, and socked me on the jaw. I reeled a little, astonished. I was also rather pleased.

I grinned at him and bellowed, 'Come on, then! Fight me! Knock my block off, if that's how you feel!' And just to aggravate him, I gave the weedy little fella a bit of a shove and he tumbled backwards against the lectern. But then he was furious and came at me with both fists flying.

Now all the audience were on their feet and there was a terrific amount of shouting going on. Everyone seemed to be arguing with everyone else – some wanting the lecture to go on in its dry old way; others relishing this more exciting debate that I had initiated.

I know, I know, my dear. I promised I would never do this again. But without your calming, restraining hand at my elbow – do you see how your George Edward Zarathustra reverts to type? Do you see how his nature is quite irrepressible? The impossible world must be made public! Everyone must know! And we scientist-adventurers must make our incredible discoveries public, no matter what the cost!

It had turned into something of a brawl, though, even I must admit. Someone had called the police, and some worried souls were starting to disperse. Yet Van Halfling and I fought on. For an elderly gent, he was wonderfully tenacious! Soon, however, Mrs Martha Danby was upon us. She had battled her way through the melee with her brolly held aloft like a flaming sword. Now she was beating the pair of us with it as we rolled on the floor, locked in fierce combat.

'Stop this at once! Desist! Both of you! You silly men! You ridiculous old sots!'

Then came the sound of sirens from outside the public library and there were running footsteps as the public disturbance dissipated around us. Van Halfling and I paused in our struggles and both decided to take heed of Mrs Danby. We were bruised, battered and our clothes were scuffed and torn. But it felt marvellous! It had been a full and frank discussion of our opposing ideologies! How dare that Danby woman think it was just a foolish brawl?

'You'd better scarper,' she advised us both. 'Before the bobbies find you.'

So that's precisely what we did.

AND SO WE RAN – THE THREE OF US – DOWN THE FRONT STEPS OF THE LIBRARY, and past those watchful lions. Somehow we summoned up enough decorum to march past the policemen as they arrived, and slipped away before we could become entangled. Mrs Danby was keeping pace with both Van Halfling and I, and it felt rather as if we were both under her schoolmarmish supervision for the duration: as if she was pinching us by the ears and leading us along.

Soon we were out on the busy city street, and hurrying ourselves through the bustling afternoon crowds towards Broadway. There was something hysterical in our behaviour, as if all three of us were longing to burst out in laughter. How shabby and ridiculous we must have looked!

It wasn't until we were almost at Times Square that anyone said anything. Of course, it was Mrs Danby, rounding on us both with an ear-bashing. 'I am ashamed of you both,' she growled, looking fiercer than I'd have thought possible under her becoming plant-pot-shaped hat. 'Abraham – this speaking tour is your livelihood now. You can't afford to mess it all up by responding to lunatic hecklers! And you!' Now she turned to me, with her eyes spewing gouts of flame. 'You have made a misery of our lives, ever since we had the misfortune to bump into you at sea! How dare you sabotage Abraham's lecture? Who are you to accuse him of intellectual cowardice?'

I was about to roar at her, my dear. I was about to give her a good drubbing for daring to quiz me thus in a public place! She, a mere housekeeper, bawling out Professor Zarathustra at the corner of the street!

However, I was interrupted by Van Halfling, who had suddenly begun to talk sense. He had seen the light, I realized. The truth of what I had driven home at the library had struck him forcibly and now he was lamenting his own want of determination.

'Zarathustra is right,' he moaned. 'I've taken quite the wrong tack with these lectures. I should be telling them the truth of what I have faced down. I should be warning them of the very real danger from the dead who walk among us!'

I clapped him on the back, and almost knocked him down. 'Good for you!' I grinned at him. 'Now you're speaking like a man of action! Not some milksop of an academic. Now! The pair of you! I have a proposition for you both!'

Mrs Danby turned on me a beseeching stare I think she hoped might dissuade me, but no luck. I continued, 'How do you both feel about accompanying me on my next dangerous quest?'

Van Halfling started to look very perturbed. We were standing by a gathering theatre queue, and were edged along the pavement. Mrs Danby shook her head firmly and told me not to be ridiculous. Nothing could prevail upon her to make her want to go anywhere with me. 'I suppose it's this magical travel agency, isn't it?' she said, in a very exhausted kind of voice. 'Well, no thank you. I've heard all about it, and I think it's all a bally con! Chinamen indeed! The planet Mars! What rot!'

Oh, she sounded so superior. I felt like taking her over my knee, I tell you. I turned on Van Halfling, 'So you told her the details of our first visit to the travel agency?'

The vampire hunter looked shame-faced. 'I saw no reason why I shouldn't. I had to share such... bizarre experiences with someone. I felt I was going mad.'

'Mad?' I boomed. 'There's nothing mad in it, sir. And I insist that you accompany me again. There is a very great secret here. An unknown kind of science or magic – I know not which, yet – behind this strange World of Mumu. It is our duty to get to the bottom of it.'

Van Halfling looked half-persuaded by this. But then the Danby woman interrupted: 'He just wants to go to that dangerous city under the sea. That's what he wants. I'll tell you what else he wants, Abraham. And that's your money! You paid last time, didn't you? You said it was expensive, that World of Mumu. Well, he hasn't got any cash, has he? He told us before. That miniature submersible of his ate up all his capital. He just wants to use you, Abraham!'

I stared at Mrs Danby and she looked triumphant. She was quite correct, of course – and all three of us knew it. But there was much more to it than that, God rot her! I valued his assistance. Van Halfling was a brave and brilliant soul – though I'd never tell him that out loud, to his face, for fear of spoiling him.

I could see the disappointment clouding his hawk-like visage. 'You just wanted my money?' he said, in a very clipped and dignified voice.

'Not just that,' I mumbled, into my beard.

But it was too late. I couldn't talk them round. The bally pair linked arms and turned in high dudgeon. They turned around and left me standing there alone on 42nd street.

I was left with no allies, no fellows in adventure, and hardly any money at all. I felt in my pockets and found a few pennies. I wandered through Times Square, rather miserably. Once again I wished you were with me, my dear.

They think me selfish. They think I only want to go to this city under the sea for the sake of my own fame and advancement. But I want to go there in order to find the Elixir of Life. Surely they can see what benefits something like that would have for mankind? Wouldn't that be worth staking everything on?

And you, my dear. You are worth staking everything on. Without the legendary elixir, you will die. We both know you have only 6 months to live and that time is ticking away; and here am I, across the other side of the world, fooling about. Failing in my quest to save you.

Perhaps if I told the others what lay at the heart of my mad scheme? Perhaps then they would understand?

But no. They hate Professor Zarathustra and all he stands for. They will never listen to my entreaties again! I have failed, my dear! Zarathustra has utterly failed in his mission! I am so sorry, my love.

EIGHTEEN
VAN HALFLING

from the journal of doctor abraham van halfling

IT DIDN'T TAKE ME SO LONG TO CONVINCE MRS MARTHA DANBY. ALTHOUGH SHE protested that she wanted nothing more to do with the supernatural, I knew that she was intrigued, despite herself, by all this talk of a travel agency that could take you anywhere in the world. She was a woman of great intelligence and imagination and she had been forced all her life to hide that beneath a mask of servitude. Naturally she would love to find out what this magical secret was, that lurked at the heart of New York City's east Village and I – Abraham Van Halfling – was the man to take her there.

What had put her off exploring this more adventurous side of her nature was that damned fool, Professor George Edward Zarathustra, who had been like a bull in a delicate shop of knick-knacks around her. Galumphing about; endangering us, almost killing us, holding us at gunpoint and generally causing the most dreadful brouhaha. His recent heckling of me for my scientific objectivism at the first of my public lectures at the New York City library and initiating a fistfight that quickly accelerated into a brawl was ghastly. Terrible man. Who could have blamed Mrs Danby – or myself – for wanting nothing more to do with the fellow? It turned out that he only wanted our help because he had no finances left, and merely wished us to bankroll his next ludicrous venture.

However, in the days that followed, and Martha – and I saw a little of each other, and explored a little more of this amazing city that never seemed to spend any time slumbering. Ach, we visited the very tops of these magnificent skyscrapers to survey the sublime views of the glittering city, and we took romantic walks along the waterfront, gazing in awe at the vast suspension bridges and the boats. I told her romantic tales of the demons I had slain and the fiends I had been forced to eviscerate in the name of all that is holy. Those were peaceful, pleasant days and – I could hardly believe it – it was possible that the two of us were perhaps falling in love.

One day, however, we were in Greenwich Village, and enjoying its quaint charms when Martha suddenly started to ask me questions about the house party I had recently attended there, where the sorcerers and magicians of Manhattan were all gathered together. Why was she interested, I wondered?

'Oh, no reason,' she smiled, pulling up the collar of her new and most becoming woollen coat and nuzzling it contemplatively. I could see the signs that she was indeed most intrigued by this idea of a cabal of wizards in Greenwich Village. Obviously that yen for investigating all that is mysterious that naturally belongs to her former employer has rubbed off on her – dear Mrs Danby!

'We could pop by there, if you liked,' I suggested. 'Ach, Henry Grenoble would be delighted to see you, I'm sure.'

'Me?' Martha asked, most demurely.

And so it proved to be true. I led her through the intricate streets and they seemed to become duskier. The gas lamps were glowing even in the middle of a spring afternoon. Scarves of some oozing kind of mist wreathed about us. We found Henry Grenoble's grand townhouse shuttered and silent, as if snoozing – but we received a warm welcome when that sinister old gent opened his front door to us.

'An honour! An honour indeed!' he cawed, like an albino crow, standing on his doorstep and gazing at Mrs Danby.

We were swept inside his porch and into that hallway filled with peculiar prints and stuffed animal heads mounted on the walls. Mrs Danby was looking about with a practised eye – though whether she was scouring the place for giveaway clues or simply a build-up of household dust, I do not know. Mr Grenoble the arch-mage bustled us into his beautiful conservatory at the back and bade his nubile Japanese servant, Rita, bring us afternoon tea.

Mrs Danby fingered the exotic leaves and petals of the plants around us. The conservatory was steamy and cloying with artificial heat that the blooms required.

'Several of these plants are toxic, Mrs Danby,' said Grenoble sharply. 'I wouldn't finger them over-enthusiastically. All of them are necessary for my spells and enchantments.'

Martha jerked her hand back and fumbled for a napkin.

'I would wash your hands, actually,' said Henry Grenoble. 'I wouldn't want you poisoning yourself. Imagine! Famed housekeeper and nautical adventuress – poisoned at the home of Greenwich Village Wizard!'

Martha smiled, but I could tell she wasn't really amused. She allowed the beautiful servant to lead her to the bathroom. Then I was alone with Grenoble.

'Where is Zarathustra?' he burst out, looking intent.

'How should I know?' I frowned. 'Ach, that terrible man. I want nothing more to do with him, after he ruined my lecture.'

'Yes, hmm, unfortunate that,' said Grenoble. 'He lets his enthusiasm get the better of him at times. I have several friends who witnessed that shameful display. You were a fool for trying to knock him out, though, Van Halfling.'

I stiffened in my wickerwork chair. 'Surely I am permitted to defend myself?'

Grenoble scowled at me. 'Zarathustra needs careful handling. He is a foolish man, but he is vulnerable. There is a great sadness about him recently. I can't put my finger on it.'

'Ach,' I retorted. 'He can go and hang.'

Grenoble looked supremely cross at my brusque, dismissive manner. He said, 'I merely ask you about him because I have not seen him for several days. Ever since he went to cause a fracas at your doomed oration, actually.'

'He has disappeared?'

'Quite possibly,' said Grenoble, ominously stirring his tea – which was very weak and fragrant. 'Ah, Mrs Danby returns.'

Here she came, divested of coat and hat, and with her hair fluffed up again. She was the very picture of mature British womanhood in her pink cardigan and tweed skirt. She sipped cautiously at her tea and let Grenoble flatter her outrageously. His blandishments and praise swept over her and she grew quite pink. Then he started boasting.

'Oh, you must give my very best to your erstwhile employer when you return to England,' said Henry Grenoble. 'Remember me to him, would you? And remind him that he and I once shared the most remarkable experience in Tibet. He was on the trail of a criminal mastermind – this would have been about 1896, I guess – and I was in the Himalayas investigating some reportedly peculiar effects that Yak butter was having on the local monks…'

His boring tales simply washed over us for some time as the afternoon sun waned over the dingy panes of glass in his rather dirty – and deadly! – conservatory. When Henry Grenoble hurried off to fetch a photograph album or some such, Mrs Danby leaned towards me and said, 'I can't see Mr Jones approving very much of this hare-brained enchanter. Yak's butter indeed. What a terrible story! And you'll never guess what I discovered in his lavatory.'

Ach, Martha Danby! What a detective! 'I dread to think,' I told her.

'I found this,' she said, and held something up for my inspection.

It was a horrid, blackened, grisly thing. 'Ach, what the devil is that?'

'It's a pterodactyl foot,' she said gravely. 'On a golden chain. I happen to know that our Professor Zarathustra never went anywhere without it. I read this in a magazine once. Ever since his adventure in the Lost World. He believes this shrivelled thing brings him wonderfully good luck.'

I declared what I knew: 'Mrs Danby – he has vanished! Grenoble just told me that he hasn't been seen for days!'

'Hmm,' said Martha, looking intent and as if she were mulling things over as intently as Mr Jones ever did. Then she took a deep slurp of her strange-tasting tea. 'Oops,' she said, and looked for a moment as if she were about to pass out. 'I do feel strange,' she added, and fell back in her chair.

I was rather concerned for my winsome companion. Though she didn't pass out or succumb to some awful form of mind control, the tea she had been given did seem to have a curious effect upon her. I asked Grenoble rather fiercely: 'What is in this filthy stuff?'

He flannelled and denied that it was anything that could do anyone harm. I realized what a fool I had been, making such a schoolboy error. One should ingest nothing when paying a visit to a Magician's house. Any idiot knows that.

Mr Grenoble was talking then, and asking me what I knew about this travel agency that Zarathustra had been so concerned with. I seemed to be in a rather loquacious mood suddenly, and I found myself telling the tale of our adventure at the agency known as World of Mumu. This man Grenoble was clearly fascinated as I described what had befallen us, and his shaggy eyebrows crept up his gleaming forehead in plain astonishment when I told him that we had been to Mars.

'Astonishing story! Amazing tale! I can hardly believe it,' he gasped, and poured us all some more tea.

Mrs Danby fixed her eyes upon him and said in a very steady voice, 'I don't trust you one bit. You are a black magician.'

'Not quite,' he smiled, very amused by her. 'Dark purple, at worst. But I'm not a bad man, truly. And I would like to help, if I can.'

Next thing – and I'm not sure how this happened – we were in the front hallway again, and his Japanese servant was helping us into our coats and outdoor things. Grenoble was donning a rather splendid cloak and looking visibly excited. 'You see,' he was saying, 'my spirit guide and my inner eye have been warning me recently. There is something afoot.'

'Something afoot?' asked Mrs Danby.

'Your inner eye?' asked I.

'Yes, yes,' said he. 'I have had intimations of something untoward. Somewhere quite close to here, the fabric of reality itself is rubbing quite thin.'

'How fascinating,' I said, feeling incredibly woozy.

'What rot,' mumbled Mrs Danby.

Then we were out on the street in Greenwich Village, and Rita the exotic home help had slammed the front door and was watching us from behind the curtains of the living room. Tendrils of cloying mist parted for us as we followed Grenoble through the shrouded streets. We knew already where we were headed, and I felt only the vaguest sensation of alarm. Did I really wish to risk my neck and my sanity by returning to World of Mumu? And could I really consent to endangering the life of this dear woman, of whom I had become so fondly attached?

We both moved along like zombies. Ach, we had been sapped of volition by something peculiar in the beverage of Henry Grenoble!

'Van Halfling,' said Grenoble, as we came to the corner of Washington Square, 'I place you in charge now. You will lead us to this special place. You have the knowledge to take us there. Now, do so.'

And I found that I couldn't help but comply and obey him. I ground my teeth together as I led our small party through the park, cutting a diagonal path to the street on the other side. Even without thinking, I could find myself through those darkening streets to the particular alleyway and warehouse. It was all imprinted upon my mind.

I tried to tell Mrs Danby that I could not help myself. She understood – that fine woman – because she was under a similar enchantment. Henry Grenoble was skipping along beside us, wringing his pallid fingers together. 'Oh, imagine,' he was saying. 'Imagine a whole corridors of doors, leading who knows where. Each one leading to your heart's desire. Just picture that! Imagine having that for yourself...'

The cool evening air was starting to revive me, I realized. Its spring chill, but also the pungent stench of the alleys and the refuse from Chinatown, heaped on the corners of the streets. All of this was conspiring to reawaken my senses. I cast a glance at Mrs Danby and saw that she was coming back into her own mind, too.

But we were already in the long, dark, twisted alleyway that Zarathustra and I had ventured into, several nights before. The same excitement I had experienced then was upon me again. The black canyon of the alleyways between warehouses enclosed us and drew us ever onwards. The slice of starry sky narrowed above us as we entered the labyrinth and moved to find the fire escape...

'Are we almost there?' Grenoble asked eagerly. 'I can sense it. My spirit guide is telling me. He's saying the place is near. The place of portals and doors to other realities... it is very close.'

'Oh yes,' I said. 'It's very close.'

Mrs Danby was peering backwards down the alleyway at this point. She swore loudly, which rather surprised me.

'What is it?' I asked breathlessly.

But I could already see where she was pointing. And what at.

At least another dozen human forms had entered the alleyway after us. And there were others homing in from the other direction. They were silent and intent: moving in formation. Cutting off our every hope of escape.

And they were coming for us.

'What the devil?' cried Henry Grenoble. 'Chinamen! We are surrounded!'

'It's the members of a tong,' said I. 'And they want to slice us into bits.'

My Dearest Nellie,

    I must write next about how we came to be transported to goodness knows where. I mean it. It's true. I suspect that the almighty knows about this place but if he does, he's the only one that does. He must have created it, like he created everywhere on Earth... but I'm not sure what he was thinking of when he did.

    Oh my dear Nellie, we truly were transported! We were flung into somewhere absolutely vile in the deepest recesses of the Earth, with absolutely no idea what would become of us.

    Chinatown reminded me, not unnaturally, of Limehouse and other unsavoury milieus in London. I remember once traipsing round that creepy place with Doctor Wilson, when Mr Nightshade Jones had gone AWOL. We found him in an opium den, having a high old time. This place was just as dank and nasty, rife with suspicion and distrust. As we crept along alleyways, deeper and deeper into the city, we were aware of hostile eyes scrutinizing us from the inscrutable darkness.

It was when we were in a particularly gloomy alley that a horde of Chinamen set upon us. They came flying out of every corner, flinging themselves at us and doing all kinds of Martial Arts. I'm afraid I let out the most ghastly scream, and the two gentlemen swung round to defend me. Abraham put up his fists, preparing to defend us by means of the Queensbury Rules, and Henry Grenoble produced from an inside pocket a lethal-looking revolver. There must have been about thirty of the deadly men, hopping about, all ready to do us in.

I truly thought we were done for, Nellie.

'Are they vampires again?' I asked Van Halfling, knowing as I did by now, that the undead make a habit of dogging his every movement.

'They seem alive enough to me,' he said grimly, and at that very moment, lashed out with his fists at one who had advanced too close.

There followed several rather intense minutes of hand-to-hand combat, involving ourselves and the Chinamen. I won't go into details, Nellie, but suffice to say, I think I acquitted myself rather well. As you know, Doctor Wilson once showed me a number of extremely useful moves with which to defend myself. I have undergone several enlightening afternoons on the sitting room carpet at 221B. I set about employing these manoeuvres here, finding myself a little rusty, but quite efficient, actually, in taking on these rascals in the alley. Both they and my companions were rather startled that I didn't cower and scream, as they might have expected a lady like myself to have done.

The fight raged on, and Henry Grenoble shot off a few warning volleys with his pistol. It was Abraham Van Halfling who got us out of hot water, however, when he realized that we had backed up against a certain fire escape. He recognized it at once as the one that led up to the fifth-storey entrance to the travel agency we were looking for. On his command, we turned and hurried up the staircase, soon clambering high above the clamorous alleyway.

At the very top we found the door and the sign that announced, 'World of Mumu'.

'They aren't following us,' noted Grenoble.

'They have shepherded us here,' Abraham pointed out. He knocked on the door with authority. 'They could have killed us if they wanted. No, they let us through. Someone wanted to make sure we came straight to this door.'

I wasn't at all convinced by this analysis of his, but had no time to debate it, since the door flew open, and there stood a Chinese man in a satin gown and a skullcap. Without a word – just a winsome, malevolent smile – he ushered us into his spartan office.

Henry Grenoble was looking about with great interest. Abraham did the gentlemanly thing and made proper introductions between us all, and Mumu bowed elaborately in my direction.

'You are here because you have chosen a destination to which you would like to travel?' asked the Travel Agent.

'Indeed not!' growled Henry Grenoble. 'We are here to find out what has become of our dear friend, Professor George Edward Zarathustra!'

I thought 'dear friend' was pushing it a bit, but he was broadly correct. Also, there was something peculiar about Grenoble just then. He was glowing somewhat. There was a nimbus of pink flame all around his diminutive form and then – blow me – but there was a third eye opening up on his forehead. Absolutely horrid, and a very unsettling thing to witness at the best of times.

'My spirit guide tells me that he has returned to this place,' said Grenoble, stepping towards the Chinaman.

'Back!' cried Mumu, throwing up both hands, and revealing the curved talons into which his fingernails were cultivated. Most impractical, I'd have thought. He too, was suffused by light. Green light was emanating from the sleeves of his gown and I had the idea that it was some kind of protective shield against his enemy's magic. 'Stay away from me, Arch Mage Grenoble!'

Ah, I thought. These two know each other.

'Look,' said Abraham, 'this is all very interesting. However, Mrs Danby and myself didn't come here this evening for a demonstration of your pyrotechnics and sorcery. Could we please sit down sensibly and discuss this?'

Mumu looked at us and immediately remembered his manners. He nodded graciously and turned to lead us to a kind of antechamber, where there were wicker chairs and a table, which was strewn with various coloured brochures and leaflets. Glad for these signs of normality, I went to sit down. Mumu offered us some jasmine tea, but we all three of us declined. I was taking no more chances with hot drinks this evening.

'You are correct in your surmise,' Mumu told us. 'Your Professor Zarathustra returned here alone, yesterday.'

'And what did you do to him, you devil?' shouted Henry Grenoble, starting to glow again. I still couldn't look at that strange mystic eye in his forehead.

'What could I do against such a forceful and brutish man?' said the Chinaman. 'What protection did I have against him? He came rushing in here, threatening me with violence and with the police. He demanded that I let him travel through one of my magic doors again, free of charge. I gather that he has rather fallen on hard times.'

'Ach, never mind that,' said Abraham. 'What happened then? Did you let him go through?'

Mumu held up both hands helplessly, waggling his sabre-like fingernails. 'I simply had to do as he commanded. He barked out his instructions, for where he wanted to go, and I had to become his humble servant.'

'Humble servant, like hell,' growled Mr Grenoble. 'You're trickier than a bag of snakes.'

I found myself speaking up. I asked, 'Did you send him... where he wanted to be?'

Mumu turned his oddly beautiful face to stare at me, Nellie. And he said, 'Oh yes. It is a remote and strange location. One I had never heard of before. In order to go there, your Professor had to share with me his knowledge of this secret city.

I was most intrigued.'

I felt my heard thudding harder. Zarathustra had told Mumu about the city under the sea! I felt that no good would come of that. Abraham and I exchanged anguished glances.

'We want to fetch him back,' said Abraham decisively.

I looked at him. Did we? Is this really what we wanted to do? Place ourselves in awful jeopardy again, for the sake of Zarathustra?

'I feel that, alone, he has gone into the midst of dreadful danger,' Abraham said. 'And he will need assistance from his friends.'

Mumu seemed to think about this, narrowing his eyes at us. 'Sorry. No can do.'

Then he withdrew into the shadows, leaving us there on the bamboo furniture. We sat there quietly for a moment, listening to the creaking of the wickerwork beneath us.

'Grenoble, how much money do you have with you?' Abraham asked, reaching for his wallet.

Grenoble was miles away, however. He was steeped in thought. 'I have a very bad feeling about this place,' he said, pointing to that ghastly magic eye in his forehead again. 'My spirit guide is telling me some very peculiar things. Apparently it's all to do with psychic energy. That's the big kick that Mumu is getting out of this place. It isn't really about the money. It's about the psychic energy that he's leeching off his customers.'

I frowned at this. 'What is psychic energy?'

Yet, apparently, there was no time to explain to a lowly housekeeper like myself. Abraham and Grenoble were suddenly chatting between themselves very busily and all I could make out were the occasional phrases to do with 'mental energies' and 'spiritual vampirism.' Nothing very reassuring at all!

Then, all of a sudden, I became aware that the bamboo furniture we were sitting on was making even more creaking noises than ever. When I looked down at my armchair I cried out in terror. The bamboo was moving, Nellie! It was twisting and moving into new configurations. It was as if it was growing with unnatural speed, and twisting itself around my arms and legs. I was being trapped and enmeshed inside a piece of woven furniture! Panicking, I struggled to get free, and suddenly saw that exactly the same thing was happening to my two companions!

'Wait! Wait!' Grenoble shouted. 'There is an enchantment upon this bamboo. The more we struggle to free ourselves, the more tenacious and twisted it will become! We simply have to relax, and not move a muscle...'

Well, Nellie, that was far easier said than done. I fought down my panic and tried to ignore the fact that I was wrapped around most inconveniently by wickerwork strong as iron.

'Mumu has trapped us!' pointed out Van Halfling. I did feel fond of the man, but he had a habit of rather melodramatically pointing out the plainly obvious.

Then the sinister Mumu issued back into the room. My two male companions wasted several minutes hurling furious epithets at him. I couldn't see the point in insulting him, frankly. We had been silly enough to park ourselves here. Given everything else, we should have known his furniture would have something of the occult about it.

Then the Chinaman was giggling at us. We must have looked quite ridiculous, it's true. His mirth incensed Henry Grenoble to the point where the Greenwich Village wizard was glowing several different shades of purple and orange all at once. He was pulsating with mystic colours, and sparks were beginning to shoot off him. They lanced through the murky air in the direction of our now-shrieking opponent. Grenoble growled and squinched up his magical eye with tremendous effort and suddenly lightning bolts were shooting out everywhere.

'Oh!' cried Abraham Van Halfling. 'He is calling upon his deepest magical resources!'

The sinister travel agent soon became aware of the hexes that were being rained down upon him. There were visions of demons and even more hideous, unearthly beings flashing through the room. Mumu stopped laughing and started to look alarmed.

'Yes! Yes! Oh, yes!' shouted Henry Grenoble. 'You never suspected how powerful a magician I truly am, did you? I could blast you to smithereens in a second!'

Mumu scowled at us, and I saw that he, too, was trapped, like us. But he was pinioned inside a mesh of living energy that Grenoble was projecting from his sinister mind's eye. Wriggle how he might, the Chinaman could not escape.

I, for one, couldn't help but think that these two magical beings were simply showing off with this battle of enchantments.

Grenoble instructed the Chinaman to free us all from the bamboo, which he quickly did, and I breathed a sigh of relief. Then he told Van Halfling to call the cops. We were going to put World of Mumu out of business for good!

As Abraham moved towards the phone, Mumu had the last laugh, even lassoed and harmless as he was. He started to giggle again, and he warned us: 'If you do that, you will never see your Professor Zarathustra ever again. Put me out of business and not only the door to the undersea city will be closed forever. Bring the police here, and I will see to it that your precious Zarathustra will be lost to you for evermore!'

TWENTY
MRS DANBY

My Dearest Nellie,

We were absolutely aghast. Here we were – my companions and myself – trapped inside a dingy office atop a warehouse in the East Village of New York, at the terrible mercy of Mumu, who ran an occult Travel agency.

The magician Henry Grenoble, Abraham Van Halfling and I were all on the trail of our missing friend, Professor Zarathustra, who had been reportedly propelled through one of the magic doors that belonged to the deadly Mumu.

It was awful. All of a sudden I was wishing quite fervently that I had kept away from all of these men, and stuck to my plans for solitary museum-visiting and gentle sight-seeing. But instead, here I was, stuck in the midst of a horrible calamity.

Van Halfling was all in favour of beating the Chinaman up. Now that we were free of the weird bamboo that had extruded itself and pinioned us, he was up on his feet and waving both bony fists around. 'You, sir, deserve a good thrashing,' he said, jogging about before the unimpressed mandarin. 'You are no better than any other vampire. Rather than the blood of the living, you thrive by living off the life energies of the minds of your victims!'

Mumu sighed. 'That is quite true, Van Halfling. That is precisely what I do. I leech away their mental energy when they travel through my magic doors. This is why I let your Zarathustra go through free of charge. Such a strong and ferociously brilliant mind as his is a delicious bonus for me!'

'That is horrible!' cried the Greenwich Village magician, Henry Grenoble. I did wish he'd close up that third eye in his forehead. I found it most disturbing. 'What becomes of them, when you drain away their mental powers?'

Mumu gave a callous shrug. 'Gradually, they weaken, and they go out of their minds. They simply fade away. That is, if they stay longer than twenty-four hours beyond the threshold of one of my magic doors. Twenty-four hours is relatively safe.'

Van Halfling stepped forward again, prepared to punch our enemy's lights out. Suddenly I found myself interceding.

'There's no use trying to fight him, Abraham,' I said. 'The blighter is holding all the cards.' Honestly, Nellie, I don't know where this new outspoken me was coming from. I sounded so forthright! Calling him a blighter, too! Doctor Wilson would have been ever so proud. 'If we beat him or call the police, then we'll never be able to drag Zarathustra back. As Mumu says, he will be lost for ever.'

'What do we do, then?' Abraham frowned. 'We can't place ourselves in his hands...'

Clever Abraham had already guessed what I was going to suggest. What did I care if Zarathustra languished forever at the bottom of the sea? Wasn't it where he was so keen on going to, anyway? He'd caused enough rumpus trying to find his way to that secret city...

But still, I simply could not stand by and allow this man with the magic doors drain away all the Professor's brain energy. And so I came up with a plan. It had been bubbling away in my mind ever since we'd been tangled up in that magic bamboo.

I told Mumu: 'You are going to send *us* through that door you sent the Professor. We are going to rescue him and you are going to help us.'

Mumu gave me a nasty smile. 'You are going after him? You must be very brave.'

'I am!' I burst out. 'We all are!' I swung round to look at Abraham. 'We've been through quite a few scrapes, haven't we, Van Halfling? We're no softies.'

Van Halfling nodded at me, and Henry Grenoble tried hard to look courageous.

'Mr Grenoble, you will stay here in the office with Mumu,' I told him. 'You will make sure that we are not betrayed. Then, Abraham and I will take the particular door that will lead us to the secret, ancient city.'

As I put this into words, I was starting to quail inside. It sounded rather daunting a task, when I actually said it aloud.

Mumu snickered. 'You will really brave this unknown city?'

'Of course,' I said. 'We can't let you drain away the life force of our friend. It's just not on.'

Mumu nodded. 'The city is called Arachnopolis. Did you know that?'

I exchanged a glance with Van Halfling. 'No, we didn't. How would we know that?'

'Oh,' said Mumu airily. 'I thought Professor Zarathustra might have told you. Yes. Arachnopolis. Do you have any idea why it might be called that?'

'None at all,' I snapped grimly. Van Halfling looked as if he had an idea or two. But I ignored his worried expression. I hadn't studied foreign or ancient languages and sometimes – especially on the brink of a dangerous adventure – ignorance can be bliss, Nellie.

Well, blow me down, but the Chinese travel agent complied. He showed us through a door at the back of the office, and into the corridor that Van Halfling had earlier described to me. A dimly-lit corridor filled with doors of all shapes, sizes, colours and materials. The corridor seemed to go on forever. We walked for several minutes, staring fascinated at everything as we went. We left Henry Grenoble and his revolver behind in the office, and I was sure that I saw a glint of relief in his eye as he assured us that he would 'take care of things at this end.'

Then Mumu suddenly came to a halt before a particular door, which was painted scarlet and gold. 'This is it,' he declared.

We both stared at him. 'Very well,' I said. 'Let us through.'

'Are you sure about this?' Mumu asked, and he had the gall to pretend to sound concerned. 'Your Professor bullied his way past me. He didn't care a fig for the consequences.'

'That sounds very much like him,' said Van Halfling.

'He never knew you were draining his psychic powers,' I say. 'He would never have gone had he known about that. He values his brain power very highly. Even above discovering unknown cities like this... this Anarch... Achron...'

'Arachnopolis,' Mumu supplied. Then he reached forward and opened the door very dramatically.

There was nothing but darkness beyond.

'What do we do?' I asked.

Van Halfling was an old hand. 'Just step through, my dear... It helps if one gives... a little hop.'

So that's what we did. And, in the instant before we hopped through that doorway into the blackness, I felt my hand slide into his. Or maybe he reached out to grab mine. Either way, we were clutching each other by the hand as we hopped through the door.

And together we experienced one of the most peculiar sensations I have ever had to give myself up to.

It was rather like falling *up* a spiral staircase, Nellie, if you can imagine such a thing. Falling up rather than down the twisting coils and turns of a spiralling staircase while some annoying person is flashing colourful lights through the darkness at you. As all of this was going on, I was dimly aware of Van Halfling shouting something at me about us passing through dimensional interstices, or something. He was still clasping my hand and we sailed along together through this realm that seemed to have no up or down, nor any real substance to it at all.

All I knew was that we had seemingly left New York far behind. That upper-storey lair of the fiend known as Mumu was a long way away by now.

We were hurtling to a new location, on the trail of our missing friend. Only now did it occur to me that the slippery chap might have sent us in quite another direction. There was nothing to hold him to his promise to send us after Zarathustra.

As a point of rapidly expanding, silvery light appeared ahead of us, I realized that we could in fact be on the point of arriving absolutely anywhere... in the whole galaxy!

During our final few seconds in that unearthly element, Van Halfling cried out something about preparing myself for a shock...

And then that luminous brightness broke over both of our heads. It was like liquid quicksilver poured over us. We squeezed our eyes tight closed and our limbs collapsed between us. Both of us rolled up tight as we fell upon the floor. But at least there was ground beneath us! At least there was fresh air in our lungs!

Actually, it wasn't so fresh. When I opened my eyes in our new environment, the first thing that struck me was its fustiness. There was something stale about the new atmosphere in which Abraham and I found ourselves sprawling. It reminded me absurdly of the smell of my Uncle's potting shed, at the bottom of his garden. What a ludicrous association to make, I thought! But... and here I sat up, and adjusted my clothing and peered around. The new place did in fact smell somewhat... dank and insecty and... *cobwebby*. Yes, that was the word.

We were both in a dark room. A tunnel. The ground and walls were lumpy and bumpy and seemed to be made from hard-packed earth. There were tatters of some greyish, sticky fabric hanging about the place...

'I don't like it at all,' I told my travelling companion. He was taking stock, and looking monumentally unimpressed. 'Where has that heinous travel agent delivered us, do you think?'

Van Halfling was picking at some of that sticky, flossy stuff on the wall. Yes, it was cobwebs, I could see that now. There were flies stuck in it, and other nasty things. I watched as Abraham Van Halfling thoughtfully put both index fingers in his ears and bugged out his eyes. Then he held his nose and pursed his lips. He seemed to be calculating something under his breath. 'I think, judging by the pressure in the air, and everything, that we are, in fact, at the bottom of the ocean. As deep as we were last week, when we were in Professor Zarathustra's miraculous submersible.'

'At the bottom of the sea!' said I, incredulously. 'But it's so dry and... earthy. And rather nasty, too.'

'Yes, it is, isn't it?' he frowned, tugging on his sideburns. 'This is it, I think. The great city that Professor Zarathustra wanted us to visit.'

I tutted. 'Typical. All of this fuss and just look at it! Gloomy old tunnelly place!'

Van Halfling shrugged and grinned at me and suddenly it didn't seem so bad. Not when I had him gallantly leading the way. Soon the tunnel was a little wider and glowing with something that Abraham called 'natural phosphorescence'. We didn't have to crouch so much. We could hear sounds of distant activity, so that we knew we were not alone here, at the very bottom of the ocean.

'But what kind of people would live in a place like this?' I wondered aloud, feeling less afraid, I think, than I would have done in my earlier life. I think I was becoming used to being on dangerous escapades, Nellie. I had developed what is known as an adventurous spirit!

Van Halfling paused then, and reached back to grip my arm. He shushed me sharply and we both listened. Yes, those were footsteps. But they were curiously light footsteps. Careful, nimble footsteps, coming from some way ahead in the

MRS DANBY AND COMPANY

gloom. And many of them.

Tap tap tap... Here they came...

'What kind of people?' Van Halfling frowned at me.

'Indeed,' I said. 'I mean, if they've been living here, on the ocean bed for goodness knows how long... why, they might be quite different from folk on the surface, like us. Why, I suppose they might even...'

Abraham was giving me a look that was full of concern and also, maybe, a touch of annoyance. He was looking at me as if I hadn't quite understood the point of something that had already been established. All around us that peculiar tapping noise was getting louder as our hosts approached.

'What?' I snapped at him.

'Martha,' he said. 'Arachnopolis. That's what the city is called. Don't say you didn't realise?'

I frowned at him. 'Do you mean it's full of anarchists?' As you know, Nellie, I take a very dim view of those.

'Anarchists?' he cried. 'My dear, the name is *Arachnopolis!* And it's full of... *spiders!*'

Well, you could have knocked me down with a feather. Because they weren't just *any* old spiders that came hurrying around that corner, out of the tunnel, with all their horrid legs and what-have-you twitching.

Oh no, Nellie. No indeed. They were great big fat *giant* spiders, weren't they? Great big giant spiders, shooting webby stuff out of their unmentionables.

That's what was coming down that filthy hallway to attack us!

TWENTY-ONE
PROFESSOR
ZARATHUSTRA

My Dear Mrs George Edward Zarathustra,

Now it is time to fill you in on some of the details of the extraordinary adventures that have befallen your husband. Since I paid my most recent visit to that nefarious Chinaman's travel agency in the East Village, I have been propelled into the most bizarre world I think I have ever visited. And that is saying something for, as you know, your husband has visited a bewildering array of exotic and dangerous lands!

Yet here I am in the City I was searching for, deep beneath the Atlantic Ocean. I made it to my impossible destination, my dear! I bullied and harangued that sinister Mumu and forced him to let me use one of his magic doors, this time free of charge. He could do nothing but cave in and give way to Professor Zarathustra's determination!

So I stepped through a certain gold and red door and found myself transported by some peculiar means to this far-distant city, which has been built beneath a green, translucent dome at the bottom of the sea. Now I see it all at close hand, I find that the dome is in fact woven from delicate strands of steel-hard webbing. Every last jot of it extruded by the city's inhabitants.

Yes, indeed! *Extruded*, my dear!

They are spiders, my love! Spiders each the size of an omnibus! Intelligent, ghastly, hairy-legged spiders, who have inhabited this city of Arachnopolis for many hundreds of years.

Oh yes, indeed – they speak English. Somehow, they can link their subtle, spidery minds to my own, and make their feelings and thoughts known to me, and I hear them in the form of almost perfect English.

Please, my dear, I hope you do not fear for me when I reveal this horrible truth about the creatures that lurk in this long-sought-for metropolis. I have so far found them to be rather amenable and welcoming hosts. Remember, I myself must have seemed a rather startling sight to them when I first popped up, right into their midst, yesterday afternoon. The spiders were having a large gathering – some kind of council meeting, I believe. The air was hot and shrill with their debating voices in a high-ceilinged chamber. And it was here that the door opened up and I staggered through. I will have to admit to being somewhat startled to be thrown in at the deep end. I mean, picture it! Rows and rows of these monstrous beings, each with multiple limbs and those shining arrays of lamp-black eyes! All staring at me! I must admit to letting out perhaps a small bark of surprise at the sight.

They were upon me at once, of course. Their guards leapt into action and shot forward to spray me with liquid webbing, which soon formed a kind of woolly and sticky cocoon about me, just as you see around a luckless fly caught in a web. Luckily, this was just a precaution and no one put me into their larder.

At least, I was assuming that the chamber I was then popped into was no one's larder. It was clean and small, but I could see no other beings – living or dead – who were waiting to be liquidized and devoured. I counselled myself that I had been merely placed in a kind of waiting room, and soon I would be introduced to someone more senior than those in the busy chamber.

Well, blow me, if I wasn't right! Several tense hours passed in that cobwebby room – I'm not sure how long I was there. Possibly I slept. Perhaps the webs that pinioned me contained some kind of drug that made me fall unconscious. After some unknowable amount of time I found myself being shaken awake by thick, hairy legs. A bushel of those glittering eyes were peering into my face and somebody with a screeching voice was telling me, 'Now you see will Queen the up wake.'

I thought it was some effect of my general doziness, but no. The Spiders have the most incredible telepathic powers, allowing them to peer into our minds and absorb our language. But for some reason they are made quite differently to us, and speak all our sentences *backwards*.

I grasped hold of this warrior spider's meaning at once. There was a Queen spider, was there? And she wanted to see me, did she? Well, naturally she did. A being such as I had arrived, all unannounced and quite spectacularly, in the heart of what appeared to be the spiders' parliament. Of course she wanted to be introduced to me.

Oh, but it was daunting at first, to be led through tall corridors and across silken bridges by these colossal beasts, my love. Something in the very soul of man cringes in instinctive dread from the form of these spiders. I had to remind myself that I am Zarathustra! I have walked among far larger and much more dangerous monsters than these!

The Queen was, however, a startling sight. Her throne room was magnificent, all coloured rock arranged in strange configurations which, when I looked more closely, seemed to depict key moments in the history of the spiders. She herself was suspended from a single, elegant silver strand of webbing. She dangled there with perfect poise. As I was urged forward to meet her, I could sense a certain... scratchiness inside my head and I knew it was her presence there, within my mind, acquiring knowledge of me and my world and my words.

'Festival the for time in arrived have you,' she told me, in a confiding tone that was rather like having very pointed nails scratching along the soft flesh of your inner arm. I realized at once that she, too, had picked up the backwards-speaking thing. How interesting, I thought, that the minds of spiders should run in the opposite direction to our own!

I tried to reply in kind. 'Welcome wonderful your for you thank.'

She stiffened and glared at me, upside down on her silver rope. 'Backwards speak you dare how!'

And I realized I had done quite the wrong thing. 'I apologise your majesty.' Then I added, 'Did you say something about it being festival time?'

She nodded and dropped a little lower, coming level with me, and staring into my eyes. 'Festival a for time is it. Husband new a chosen have I.'

'Congratulations, Your Majesty,' said I, glad that I was picking up the gist of her strange backwards speech. Around us, the other giant spiders in attendance were applauding politely. Very odd thing it is, to see spiders clapping their skinny, sticky limbs together. Oh, but they were rapt with interest. This seemed to be a very important moment to them.

'Husband new my be will you,' she said, grandly.

At first I thought she was asking me. But she wasn't. She was informing me.

'Well, of course, I'm very flattered...' I stammered. Was such a thing even legal, I wondered? For a man to marry an arachnid lady? Even one as highly intelligent as she? Besides, I already have a wonderful human wife! I had no desire to be clasped to the hard bosom of his creature!

'I am afraid I must turn down your marvellous offer!' I announced, with all due ceremony.

The Queen dropped lightly to the ground and glared at me. 'No,' she said. 'Possible not. Refusal no be can there. Now be must it. Here be must it. Festival the is it. You marry will I. You with mate will I and.'

'Oh,' I said. 'Me with mate will you?'

She nodded hungrily, drooling upside down. 'You with mate will I. Watching be will everyone.'

I hope you will forgive me, my dear, for being paid court to, so elaborately, by another lady. I hope you will see, Mrs Zarathustra, that I had no choice in the matter and besides, having heard the details of her proposal, I wasn't at all keen.

Then there began the most horrendous cacophony, and it took me some moments to realise that this was the spidery equivalent of celebratory music. They had fetched out weirdly-shaped instruments of all kinds, and were sawing away at strings made out of tautened webbing. It was a very uncanny noise that filled my ears as I was installed on a small throne beside the preening Queen. As I sat there and watched these creatures entertaining themselves, I experienced a sudden rush of despair. The kind of thing that you know I am not usually given to. But for once I couldn't see any way out of this. These spiders were much too strong for me. It seemed only too inevitable that I would be married and mated with, in quick succession, if I didn't come up with a useful plan pretty sharpish. I needed to focus my mind.

Time moved very oddly in the city of the spiders. Was it a whole evening that I sat there, stewing over my predicament? Certainly, the horrid music seemed to last a lifetime. The Queen amused herself by sliding up and down her ropes of silken webbing. My blood crawled as she came close to her intended, and I felt the tips of her limbs stroking my head or fondling my hair. She brushed me gently, and absent-mindedly as a ghastly feast was brought round for the court of spiders. Giant flies, mummified and baked in cobwebs. I sat still and struggled manfully to retain my composure. I was determined that my final meal as an undefiled and happily married man would not be desiccated insect.

And then, after what seemed like a lifetime of these ghoulish festivities, there came an alteration in the atmosphere of the place. A ripple of amusement went around the large chamber. A soldier brought the queen a titbit of news.

Eavesdropping, I learned a little of what was going on. I heard the words 'intruders' and 'beings human'. The Queen fixed her glassy stare on me and asked, 'Mumu of World of doors the through you followed have friends your seems it.'

It took me a moment to puzzle out what she meant. Friends? Followed me here? I frowned. What friends had I? I wondered mournfully. None! None in all of New York City! Hardly any in all the world! 'Your Majesty,' I protested. 'No one would care about me passing through that door to come here. No one even knows!'

No one apart from the wretched Mumu himself, I thought. And then another thought struck me. How curious it was that the undersea monarch of Arachnopolis should know a Manhattan travel agent by name? Was the Queen of the Spiders really on first-name terms with that nefarious Chinaman?

However, my speculations were cut rather short then, by a kerfuffle in the throne room. Soldiers were herding these new intruders into our midst. The soldiers were terrifying beasts, crouched tensely, bristling with armaments. They strode purposefully into the room, bringing with them two diminutive human figures. Two figures all too familiar to me.

I was on my feet at once. 'Van Halfling! Mrs Danby! You came after me! I can hardly believe it!'

You will think old Zarathustra a fool for wiping away a sentimental tear. But really, I could hardly help myself, my dear. To think that these two could bring themselves to forgive all the bother I had already caused them! To think that they had managed to find a way to come after me, having perceived – rightly, as it turns out – that I would have found myself in horrible danger.

'There you are, old chap!' Doctor Van Halfling called out, looking every inch a gentleman in his evening dress. His voice rang with confidence and authority, even in this filthy place.

Mrs Danby looked rather less certain of herself. Her discomfort had less to do with a housekeeper's professional hatred of spiders and cobwebs than it did sheer, stark, raving terror. She simply stared at me in my place beside the Queen, who was chuckling, nastily, and drooling hungrily. Her saliva was cold and it was going down my neck, but I managed not to protest.

'A-are you well, Professor Zarathustra?' stammered Mrs Danby, in the tone of one thrust into unwelcome company at an unconvivial party.

'So far, yes,' I called back. 'Though I am a hostage. Her Majesty here has promised to marry me and perform her conjugal rites upon my person.'

'Good God!' exclaimed Van Halfling. 'But aren't you already married?'

I was gratified to find that the many hundreds of eyes of the court were upon us. We were the centre of everyone's attention in that most lofty of settings within the secret city. 'That is a true fact, my dear Van Halfling,' I told him. 'And it seems that I have no choice in the matter. The Queen has rather taken a fancy to me.' All at once I felt a blood-rush of indignation. A red mist suffused my vision. I stood up, refusing to be bowed beneath their intimidation. 'And why should she not fall in love with Zarathustra? Would not most ladies in the world trade places with her and coerce Zarathustra into unholy wedlock? Is he not the most brilliant and well-developed male specimen in the British Empire?'

I distinctly heard Mrs Danby let out a noise halfway between a deep sigh and a groan. I believe she was swooning at my words.

'However,' and here I turned gruffly towards my foul oppressor. I imagined those jewel-like eyes of hers were swimming with tears. 'I cannot go to you, my dear Queen. For I am already taken. Mrs George Edward Zarathustra, of Greenwich, London, England, is already my bride and I will take no other. Or, er, be taken by no other.'

The Queen paused a moment. She gave me a rather hard stare.

'Nevertheless you marry will I. You with mate will I. You devour will I finally and.'

I stared back at her. 'Me devour will you?' I gasped.

'Yes, oh,' said the Queen of Spiders.

TWENTY-TWO
MRS DANBY

My Dearest Nellie,

It is no exaggeration to say that I had been pitched into the midst of the most horrible nightmare. Back in the office of Mumu in New York, it had seemed somehow possible that Abraham Van Halfling and I could pursue Professor Zarathustra through the magic door. It would be a relatively straightforward matter – we fondly thought – to catch up with him and rescue him from this undersea city of Arachnopolis.

What were we thinking of?

Well, obviously we hadn't reckoned on the place being inhabited by highly intelligent spiders the size of hansom cabs. Would you credit it, my dear? This long-sought destination hankered after by the self-proclaimed greatest explorer-scientist-adventurer of his age turns out to be the home of the most grotesque monsters you or I could possibly imagine.

There we were, Van Halfling and I, newly-arrived and captured by the long-legged behemoths, and standing together in the gloomy magnificence of a throne room. It belonged to the nastiest looking insect of the lot – the Spider Queen.

'Strictly speaking, spiders are not insects,' Abraham Van Halfling kindly informed me.

I let him know that I didn't really care about their correct classification, hissing back at him out of the corner of my mouth. I was more concerned by the fact that they had Zarathustra bundled up in wads of webbing, and the Queen had announced her intention to do several quite nasty things to him, as part of their ritual celebrations, in the none-too distant future.

'Yes, most unfortunate, that,' Van Halfling winced. 'One can hardly appreciate how such indignities could even be possible.'

The Queen scowled at us from the silver threads she had spun for herself. I couldn't at first understand a word of her sibilant, salivary speech. It seemed to be a corrupted form of English, and Van Halfling told me that the reason for that was that she was able to read our minds, partially. A fact which I found less than reassuring. If she could read my mind I am sure she'd see all the occasions I'd extinguished the lives of her surface-dwelling brethren, with shoe heels and rolled-up newspapers.

Servants came to put us in some horrible kind of cell. To my surprise they seemed at first sight to be human beings that came shuffling in to do her bidding, but they weren't, as it turned out. They were blue-skinned and gilled, with bulbous, golden eyes. 'My goodness!' Van Halfling exclaimed, and he couldn't keep the excitement out of his voice. 'Amphibian people!'

I'm afraid it wasn't the kind of thing I can get worked up about. We were taken away and locked up by these fellows who looked rather like newts or frogs and, soon after we were installed, they brought in Professor Zarathustra to keep us company. He had been freed somewhat of that cocoon of webbing, but he was still covered with tufts of the stuff, and obviously under the influence of a sedative of some kind. We embraced him, nevertheless, and he returned to a modicum of normality after some minutes.

'This is something of a disaster,' he admitted, rubbing at his beard.

Van Halfling was examining every inch of the rock-walled prison, looking for any possible means of escape. The rock was damp and, in places, running with salt water. It was a reminder that, just outside the city, were the gloomy depths of the Atlantic Ocean.

Just then, Nellie, I was longing for my bed on the seventeenth floor of the Wellington Hotel on Seventh Avenue. But that seemed just as far away as my cosy old room at the top of 221B Balcombe Street. In fact, geographically speaking, that was probably exactly true. I felt like lying down on the nasty floor, giving up and expiring on the spot.

Yet that was no good!

'How long have we got?' I asked Zarathustra. 'Until the ceremonials begin, I mean?'

He was wearing a haunted expression. 'Until she marries me?' he sighed. 'And mates with me? And devours me? In front of all her people?'

I nodded. 'She must have given you an idea about when this would all happen.'

'I don't think they work from the same clock as do we,' mused Van Halfling. 'And things like day and night must mean little to subaqueous arachnids.'

'She can't eat me!' Now Zarathustra was starting to boom again. I took this as a good sign. Perhaps he was recovering his usual spirit. 'She said that she is especially looking forward to eating my brain! Zarathustra's brain! The greatest mind of his generation! Turned to consommé by spider venom and sucked up in a trice on the whim of a queen!'

Van Halfling was stroking his sideburns very thoughtfully. 'I wonder why she particularly wants your brain.'

'Oh, that's easy,' sighed Zarathustra. 'By making a meal of my brain, she intends to inherit all my incredible knowledge.'

'What?' said Abraham. 'Can she do that?'

'Apparently,' said the Professor. 'And she wants to learn everything she can about the human race and life on the surface of our world.'

'But whatever for?' I asked. 'What do they care about our world?' But already I had a funny, cold feeling as I asked this.

'Our arrival here has been very timely, apparently,' said Zarathustra. 'We will provide them with vital knowledge about the world – just as they prepare themselves to emerge from their underground hiding chambers – and take over the whole planet!'

There was a distinct pause.

'The *fiends*,' commented Van Halfling, with a little cough. 'We must make sure we tell them that such a thing will never happen.'

'Quite,' said Zarathustra.

Then we were alerted to something strange going on in the turbid air between us. A patch of illumination grew in size and intensity. It reminded me a little of the magical hexes and spells thrown at one another by Mumu and Henry Grenoble and, sure enough, the light solidified into a three-dimensional image of the face of the Arch Mage of Greenwich Village. I shuddered at the sight of Henry Grenoble's visage, for the mystic had his third eye plainly on show again.

He spoke across the fathomless distance: 'Can you guys hear me?'

We stood before him in shock. 'Yes! Yes! We can hear!' bellowed Zarathustra. I could sense his rising excitement. He thought we were about to be rescued through means of Grenoble's diabolical sorcery. 'Hello, my good friend Henry! You have come to us just in time!'

'I only have a few seconds to talk to you,' said the phantom head of the magician. 'The mental energy it takes to project this image to where you are is impossible to maintain for long. I wanted to give you the news from this end.'

'What news, Henry?' asked Van Halfling, intercepting another of Zarathustra's time-consuming expostulations.

'It ain't good news from this end,' Grenoble sighed. 'Mumu tricked me. I was knocked out cold, just after you lot left through the magic door. And when I woke up, I was down in the alley. I'd been roughed up and robbed. And the worst of it was, when I looked up the fire escape again, Mumu and his whole office had simply disappeared. The World of Mumu has vanished into thin air.'

'What?' I gasped, horrified as we all were. We all knew what this meant.

'Gone?' cried Zarathustra. 'Did you try breaking back in?'

'Of course,' said Grenoble. 'And when I did, the rooms were dark and abandoned. And the corridor that had been filled with magic doors was completely empty. Not a door in sight. You know what this means, don't you?'

'There's no way back,' I whispered. 'We're stuck in Arachnopolis, and there's no way back to New York!'

'I'm sorry, guys,' said the magician, with all three of his eyes going misty.

'Wait! Before you go,' Zarathustra burst. 'The Queen here mentioned the World of Mumu by name. Do you think they could have been working together somehow? Something all to do with invading the world? Do you perhaps think Mumu knew about Arachnopolis the whole way along?'

Van Halfling shook his head. 'It's no good, Zarathustra. He can't hear you.'

Indeed, the distressed-looking Henry Grenoble was fading away, and soon he was just a smear of misty brightness on the air. Then that, too, was gone. Zarathustra swore loudly and at great length.

Abraham became practical and resolute. 'We are on our own. We must take responsibility for our own destinies, since there are to be no miraculous rescue attempts.'

'What do you suggest we do?' I asked.

The first suggestion was to attempt a violent breakout. Zarathustra had to pretend to be ill, and the guards opened the door to check he wasn't about to expire on them. Then Van Halfling and I were to overpower the humanoid guards. This all went rather well, up to a point. Zarathustra produced some marvellous agonized groans, which brought the froglike guards running. They clearly didn't want anything untoward happening to the Queen's intended husband and supper. And, it turns out, agitated amphibians are no match for a sock in the jaw from Abraham Van Halfling.

Then we were free to flee our poky cell, supporting the bulky form of Zarathustra between us. The Professor was muttering deliriously, and I thought I caught him still musing on this business of the spiders' possible connection to Mumu. Could they, too, be in possession of the same threshold technology as the Chinaman? Threshold technology, I wondered? I supposed he meant the magic doors.

Of course, though Van Halfling always makes a good fist of seeming competently in charge, we none of us had any idea where we were going in these dingy corridors. Soon we were hopelessly lost. We had to creep gingerly across a swaying rope bridge across a ghastly cavern, and we found the other side just as bewilderingly labyrinthine as where we'd started out.

'We're wandering around in circles,' I protested, exhausted. 'How will we ever find our way out? And,' I added, succumbing to uncharacteristic despair, 'what's even out there anyway? What can we even escape into? The bottom of the ocean? We'll drown! And that will be an end to it!'

'Hold hard,' said Van Halfling encouragingly. I must admit, I did find his demeanour in these most trying times rather reassuring. In the everyday world he could be a doddering old thing, but when the chips were down, he took on a whole new aspect.

Then, all of a sudden, the giant spiders were upon us again.

They had tracked us down as we attempted our futile escape. Van Halfling produced a swordstick and Zarathustra was waggling his pistol about again. He blew a number of spiders' legs off, which caused a terrific amount of shrill, panicked noise. Greenish ichor sprayed about the place. The spiders became very angry after that, and the battle became nastier. Van Halfling lashed out with swordstick, knives, stakes – everything he had about his person. I covered my eyes when I saw him staking the largest of the spiders' directly in the largest of his eyes.

Horrible battle!

But we were doomed. For there were an infinite number of spiders in the city of Arachnopolis. It was only a matter of minutes before the surface-dwellers tired themselves out and fresh spider soldiers came clambering angrily over the fallen bodies of their brethren to haul us away.

Dripping with green and purple blood, and sticky with sprayed cobwebs, the three of us were dragged back to the queen's throne room. It was completely hopeless, it seemed. Zarathustra fell quite silent. Obviously girding his loins for what now seemed utterly inevitable.

The Queen was incensed.

She started letting us know at quite a loud volume about what we had done. What had she done but offered us the highest of honours? She was prepared to take one of us as her very own during the holiest of her festivals. The consumption of Professor Zarathustra was a very great boon that she was bestowing upon us – couldn't we see? By trying to escape and generally massacring her minions, we were throwing her ineffable favours back into her face.

Of course, I had to concentrate rather hard to make out what the leggy monarch was actually saying, what with her saying all the words in each sentence the wrong way round. I still wasn't clear on what the reason for that was, actually. But it was while she was rambling in this maniacal way, and my two male companions were hanging their heads in what seemed to be horrified resignation, that I had my sudden brainwave.

'Your Majesty!' I burst out.

'Me with speak will you?' she spat.

'Yes, I will,' I said, very calmly, and politely, and loudly, too, so that the whole court of spiders could hear. 'We know what you are planning to do! We know that you are intending to invade and take over our world!'

'So?' said the Queen. Sentences of one word only came out the right way round, of course.

'Well,' I said, 'We won't let you get away with it.'

'You?' said the Queen. 'Army whose and you?'

I folded my arms and looked her dead in her many eyes. 'We three for a start. You're not spoiling the world we know. We won't let you. We're going to stop you! Whatever it takes! Van Halfling, Zarathustra and I!'

TWENTY-THREE
PROFESSOR
ZARATHUSTRA

To my Darling Wife, Mrs George Edward Zarathustra,

My dashed brain! It was my brilliant brain that was to be the undoing of all mankind! The Queen of the Spiders had made it all too clear, my dear, that the contents of your husband's mind would be the key to complete arachnid domination of the surface of the world and the subordination of humankind! Only through the absorbing of my brain cells could she achieve such a thing!

The grisly ruler of the undersea city had announced her plans to make a bigamist of me, then assault me in the most ghastly fashion possible, and then imbibe my liquidized brain matter during the height of her nasty ceremonials. This was an honour that Zarathustra found no relish in, I can assure you, my dear!

I had attempted to break out of that terrible place. Taking my two elderly companions under my protective wing, I had fought my way out of imprisonment. I had done battle with the horrific creatures who meant me ill. But we were hopelessly outnumbered and soon brought before the Queen again. All at once I was momentarily out of inspiration for finding the means to overcome the odds. This gave Mrs Danby the chance to surge forward and address the Queen. I could see even worse disaster looming as that woman opened her mouth.

However, she turned out to be rather persuasive. She kept a calm head and started to tell the Queen all about the surface of this world that she intended to invade. She gave her what I believe is termed a few home truths.

The Queen's several eyes opened wider as Mrs Danby told her about the monsters and maniacs at large upon the Earth. Surely the excellent woman was making some of these things up, I thought, as she went on. Then she was exhorting Doctor Van Halfling to tell all about the fiends and nightmare creatures that he encountered on a day-to-day basis. Then I was called upon to explain some of the hair-raising encounters that I have had with some of the world's more inconvenient beings.

The Queen of the Spiders listened patiently – as did her whole court – to our accounts of what the world upstairs was like. We were keen to demonstrate that it wasn't some paradisiacal place stuffed with pliant and edible humans. Conquering the world and all its denizens would be a chore for even the most indestructible of giant spiders. Even the most well-informed of giant spiders.

The Queen said something – in a shrill voice – about the above-world seeming less of an alluring place – if it truly was inhabited by the likes of the vampires, pick-pockets, burglars and dinosaurs that we all claimed. She had hoped for an easier time of it as she and her fellows rampaged about. Now she was hearing that the weather wasn't all that she could have hoped for, too. Bravo, Mrs Danby, for putting her off her stroke!

I asked, tentatively, 'So will you change your plans, your majesty? Have we dissuaded you from conquering the human world?'

The Queen flashed her eyes at me and looked surprised. 'Not course of!' she shrieked. And all our three hearts sank as we watched her limbs twitching neurotically. She stared at us blazingly, still upside down.

Then she told us that, if anything, what we had imparted had made her all the more determined to take over the world. It sounded simply delightful. But perhaps she would need extra foreknowledge and extra precautions.

I winced, guessing at what was coming next.

And, sure enough, she announced that – to be on the safe side – she would be taking two husbands. She would have Van Halfling, too, even though he was far less of an attractive prospect than I. She would be pleased to devour his brains, as well as mine, in order to supplement her knowledge.

Van Halfling looked rather queasy as the Queen started inching down her silken rope towards us. Advancing hungrily.

That excellent Mrs Danby put in quickly, in order to distract her, 'Well, what about me? Will you eat my brain, too?'

Didn't the household domestic look somewhat put out then, when the Queen threw back her head and laughed? The whole chamber rang with callous laughter. The entire court joined in and Mrs Danby blushed with shame. But really, what did she expect? What would the Queen of Arachnopolis ever want with the contents of Mrs Danby's head? Ridiculous woman!

After her shrieking laughter subsided, the Queen darted forward and told Mrs Danby that she would remain intact. And she would have the honour of accompanying the spidery hordes up to the surface as they conquered the world! Some kind of messenger or go-between was bound to be necessary and Mrs Danby would fit that bill nicely. The housekeeper looked crestfallen and sick with dread.

Then, before sending us off to be scrubbed and smartened up for the ceremonials (we were, in fact, not at our tidiest, it must be said), the Queen said something rather queer. Something that had me thinking rather dark thoughts. She said that Van Halfling and I were lucky. In being consumed by the Queen of Spiders, we would find a curious kind of immortality. The promised immortality of the ancient gods of Arachnopolis.

Then she dismissed us, into the waiting hands of her amphibious servants, and we were taken off to be scrubbed and prepared.

Those dark thoughts went churning through my head, my dear, so that I was hardly aware of all that befell me during the next hour or so. Immortality, my dear! The secrets of the undersea gods!

Van Halfling was burbling about the queen and how he suspected that she spoke backwards because, although she could read our minds, she was hanging upside down. And so perhaps she was reading them right to left rather than the more usual way around?

He could be a fool sometimes. Mrs Danby and I weren't interested in his theories of language acquisition or telepathy. We were meditating on our own fates and discoveries. Chief among these thoughts, and more important than any, was my realization about immortality.

'There is no elixir!' I gasped, desolately. 'The inscription in the old Mayan tombs had it wrong! The whispered rumours and hearsay of a dozen centuries... all of it wrong, wrong, wrong!'

Mrs Danby looked at me, covering up her modesty as the amphibious people scrubbed at both of our skins. 'What's that? What are you on about now?'

'No prize of immortality!' I wailed, almost drowning in the suds and cleansing foam. 'Didn't you hear her? The only immortality they know about down here is in the Queen's mind. She eats her victims and absorbs their knowledge, and so they live on inside her monstrous head. Such will be my only reward for my determination! Such an abomination lies at the heart of my quest!'

Mrs Danby shrugged. 'Well, never mind.'

Van Halfling glowered across the hot tub. 'Immortality. Pah. What a terrible thing. You should be glad, Zarathustra. We should all be glad that it was a chimera. The immortal creatures I have met have all been accursed.'

But... But... But...! And here I fell silent, my dear. I could not tell them the truth about why I had been searching for the mythical elixir. They wouldn't understand. Or even if they did, I wouldn't want their pity. I wanted the secret of eternal life for *you*, Mrs George Edward Zarathustra. But I have staked our hopes and dreams on the wrong goal. I have failed ignominiously, my dear. I cannot save your precious life.

And now the whole world is about to be taken over by the spidery hordes.

Things are not looking particularly good.

Even Professor Zarathustra must learn to admit defeat as it overtakes him.

From down those intricate and cobwebby tunnels we could hear the nasty festivities stepping up a pace. The music was horrid and quite alien to our ears. My throat went dry at the thought of what was about to befall Van Halfling and myself, and no amount of pep-talk from Mrs Danby could stir us from our gloom and dread. It wasn't so much the brain-feeding that I was in fear of. It was the thought of the nuptials which would precede it that made me shiver.

But then, something happened.

Hurrah!

I should have known! Something always turns up, does it not? Some unexpected twist or turnabout in my fortunes? It's as if the universe itself doesn't want Zarathustra to die! As if the benign spirit of the world intercedes occasionally in my affairs to see that nothing bad overcomes me.

This time that unsuspected benevolence came in the form of one of our amphibious guides. Moy, he was called. A newt-like creature who brought back our clothes to us, completely cleaned and pressed, so that we suddenly looked just as spick and span as we had done seemingly months ago when we were in New York. Moy bowed to us in supplication and treated us kindly and, through a minimum of words and gestures, let it be known that he and his fellows – who all belonged to the servant class in Arachnopolis – did not at all approve of the way the spiderkind had treated us. And they were mortified by the Queen's proposed plans for invading the world above. The amphibians could only guess that such upheavals would portend dire consequences for all of us.

Mrs Danby, Van Halfling and I were only too glad to encounter such a sympathetic being. Once we were arrayed in our fresh clothing, this Moy person – along with his quiescent and blue-skinned chums – allowed us to slip out of our imprisonment. We were led swiftly through some of the undersea dome's obscurer passageways and it was with relief that we realized that the music of the spiders' celebrations was fading away into the distance.

Together we came to the very outskirts of the city, and gazed up at the magnificent structures that our nemeses had built. Malignant they may be, but the spiders had woven something very impressive. It might well have been one of the lost wonders of the world, that vast and semi-permeable dome that stretched over the towers and slender spires of Arachnopolis. Through its glaucous transparency we could see the vast deeps of the ocean and it made us think that perhaps there was some way of escaping the clutches of the spiders and travelling home again...

Though, it has to be said, Mrs Danby looked rather bilious at the sight of all that dark water. No natural sailor she, I think.

Moy led us through shadowy, flickering galleries in the city of the spiders. He told us a little about the history of his people and how they had been servants for thousands of years. He told of how the spiders took them over and made them work, and of the strange technology that the spider masters are possessed of. How it allowed them to live under water and dabble with travel through separate dimensions.

'Threshold technology!' I cried. 'So it is the spiders who created the magic doors in the first place?'

Moy wasn't so sure about that. He said that no one really knew where the magic doors came from, and no one could control them entirely. But the Spider Queen and her devilish hordes knew enough to make good use of them. With the knowledge of the human world that we had brought to Arachnopolis, Moy feared that the spiders would now prove to be unbeatable.

Mrs Danby went all tender-hearted then. She even patted the slimy-skinned fellow on his shoulder, asking whether he shouldn't be pleased? If the spiders invaded New York and the whole human world above, then maybe Moy and his own people would be left alone for once?

But the newt-like man wouldn't believe it. He was a bit of a pessimistic sort, all in all, I thought.

Van Halfling ventured his own ha'penny worth then, chewing on his sideburns contemplatively and saying, 'Well, if these spider chappies have had this threshold technology business for such a long time, then how come they haven't invaded the world before, hmm? How come we above ground have never heard of the bounders?'

I burst out in a shout of bitter triumph then. They all looked at me expectantly.

'Why, the answer is obvious, is it not?' I bellowed at them. 'The spiders have surely been waiting for me, haven't they?'

Mrs Danby groaned aloud at the obviousness of it, now that I had pointed it out to her.

I went on, 'Remember how I was plagued with images of this city? How I believed I longed to find this city, in order to discover the secret of immortality?'

'Yes,' said Van Halfling drily. 'I believe we were made aware of that fact.'

'It was a noble quest! One that would reap many benefits for mankind as a whole and for others, too. But these ideas and thoughts were planted oh-so insidiously in my brain. The Spider Queen drew me here, encouraging me to find this place, and to bring my knowledge to her. It is me that they need! It is Professor Zarathustra's mature genius that the spiders require!'

The amphibian Moy, Van Halfling and Mrs Danby all stared at me. Mrs Danby simply said, 'Is that a fact?'

The impact of this truly nefarious scheme took a few moments for each in our small band to absorb.

Then I told them, 'Nevertheless, we must all face together what seems so inevitable now. It seems an invasion of the world we hold dear by giant spiders is almost upon us. Unless...! Unless Professor Zarathustra can come up with something completely brilliant! And save the whole world!'

They all looked at me.

'Go on then,' said Van Halfling.

I looked back at them, somewhat crestfallen. 'I have absolutely no ideas!'

Then Moy spoke. 'There is a way to defeat the spiders. But be warned... for it could cost you your minds!'

TWENTY-FOUR
VAN HALFLING

from the journal of doctor abraham van halfling

THIS WAS QUITE A PICKLE WHICH WE HAD GOT OURSELVES INTO, AND NO MISTAKE.

Amidst all the melodrama, adventure and excitement in which we were embroiled – i.e. escaping and being captured by the Giant Undersea Spiders of Arachnopolis – we were also learning rather a lot about their peculiar and exotic civilization down there at the bottom of the ocean. We discovered that they ruled over an underclass of amphibious humanoid beings, who were the original inhabitants of this region of the ocean bed. We had made a particular friend and ally of one of these beings, who was called Moy.

This very civilized young chap told us a number of secrets to do with his people, and those daemonic spiders, and all of his information was terribly useful to us. For there we were – Professor Zarathustra, Mrs Danby and my good self – on the run from the arachnids, and all too aware that we were the only ones who stood between our many-legged captors and their aim of enslaving the whole human world. Ach, what a day it was.

Mrs Danby – I was gratified to note – was rather stoical and brave when the chips were down quite as emphatically as they currently were. Professor Zarathustra was, I must admit, a terrific disappointment. He had become rather hysterical. It was he, after all, whom the Spider Queen particularly wanted to copulate with and this seemed to exercise his nerves more than even the thought of being devoured. As we fled to the city's outskirts under Moy's expert guidance, Zarathustra was gabbling like a man possessed about how we might spoil the spiders' plans, or otherwise poke a stick in the spokes of their machinations. He was also ranting about how he presumed himself to be the reason the spiders felt able to attack humankind and so on and so on. He was building up his part, as per usual, and puffing up his – in my experience – rather frail ego.

He was still carrying on in this shameful manner when Moy showed us to a particularly striking chamber. Its walls – though constructed of the same steel-like webbing of which most of the city was composed – were nevertheless transparent. We could see out into an endless, watery vista. Here and there we could see serpents and colossal fishy beings slithering and gliding. It was most impressive, I thought.

Mrs Danby didn't like the look of it at all. Professor Zarathustra pretended that his scientific curiosity was aroused, but I could tell that his mind was still scrambled by incipient panic.

Then the amphibian man known as Moy showed us through a doorway into an ante-chamber composed of some beautiful, mesmerizing crystal. He let it be known that this was, to his people, one of their holy of holies, and we three were honoured indeed to be shown it. All three of us held our breaths in astonishment as we stood inside that crystal cave. The interior dimensions were deceptive in the quicksilver flash of reflections. It hurt one's eyes just to stand there for too long.

'It's beautiful,' gasped Mrs Danby. 'But, forgive me, Moy... Why are you showing us this place?'

I must admit, the same question was plaguing me, too. And I was very glad of Moy's candid reply.

'Many hundreds of years ago,' he began, in a wavering, faraway voice. 'My ancestors were masters of their domain. They ruled wisely and well. They lived in harmony with the sea beasts and the monsters of the deep, the likes of which I believe you people have already encountered on your recent adventures.'

'Not half,' mumbled Mrs Danby, under her breath.

'Ah, the ghastly cephalopods!' sighed Zarathustra. 'Did I tell you how I fought one in hand to tentacle combat?'

I shook my head at him. Now really wasn't the time. Moy had something to tell us. Something which, I felt sure, was going to prove germane to tackling our immediate concerns.

'The behemoths of our undersea kingdom – and the smaller creatures, too – helped us in cultivating and harvesting the seabed. We worked together harmoniously to our mutual benefit. But all of that was ruined by the coming of the spiders, some thousand years ago. They arrived using their Threshold technology and soon took charge. Meting out death and torture, they forced us to help them build cities in vast bubbles filled with air. They colonized us. They ruined our lands. And they took control of the means by which we communicated with the beasts of the ocean.'

Moy went on to explain to us how, through the vast, central city of Arachnopolis, there were several crystal caves like this one, hidden away. The spiders had learned that the crystals were the key to controlling the serpents and giant fish. The crystals had been used since time immemorial by the amphibians to amplify their thoughts and to receive those of the beasts. When the spiders learned of this, and how to work this most peculiar variation on a wireless set, they ruthlessly took it over. They amplified their own horrible thoughts a millionfold, and sent out waves of malign mental interference – enslaving both amphibians and sea creatures alike.

'So that is how the octopi were being controlled,' said Mrs Danby, grasping the truth at once. 'They were really were being sent out to guard this place against discovery!'

'Indeed not,' cried Zarathustra. 'They were coming for me! The octopi attacked because they knew I was near! They came to drag me down to see the Queen of the Spiders!'

I'm afraid I shushed him quiet then, for I had many urgent questions for our cooperative, froglike companion. 'This fires my imagination most keenly,' I admitted. 'For whoever wields power over this cave of crystal stands to cause great upheavals in this place. Why, if one of us, say, could tap into the power held within this small, glittering antechamber, then we may set about reversing our fortunes indeed!'

Mrs Martha Danby stared at me open mouthed. 'What a brilliant idea!' she said. 'You are a most brilliant man.'

Professor Zarathustra was looking cross. 'Only Zarathustra, surely, has the requisite mental energies!'

Moy stepped forward, very politely. 'It would need to be a thinker of great subtlety and verve. The crystals can refract and bounce back wayward energies. It took the spiders many years to harness these powers. Many of their kind were killed – their minds obliterated – in the early attempts. And, alas, my own kind have been too weakened by centuries of slavery. We have tried to operate this system again but our mental strength is much too feeble...'

We thought about this. It felt like something stupendous had been offered to us – some amazing chance at escape – only to be whisked away from us, shortly afterwards.

Martha turned to me. Her green eyes were soft and moist with tears. Ach, I thought. How could I let her down? Now when she was tender with such burgeoning feelings for me?

'You can do this, Abraham,' she said. 'I know you can.'

And the extraordinary thing was, I found myself giving full sway to my feelings for her, too. Who would have thought such a thing? Such a commonplace London housekeeper. Like a brown little sparrow. Perhaps the element of danger had disturbed my equilibrium and altered my emotional responses? And yet I had been in danger before without falling in love with the woman closest to hand. No, it seems that there was some genuine kind of fellow feeling developing between we two.

Zarathustra gave an harrumphing cough. 'If you feel you fancy a stab at it, Van Halfling, then don't mind me, eh?'

I blinked at him. 'Pardon?'

'This telepathy malarkey. Focusing your mind and so on. Obviously, in the ordinary run of things, my own mind might prove the stronger – but I'm feeling somewhat fatigued after my incarceration here. I have been here longer than the two of you, remember. So – if you fancy your chances in the driver's seat – you jolly well have a go at it, old chap.'

I gave the man my most withering look. At that precise moment I'd have been quite glad to observe what the Queen Spider might have in store for him. Except, of course, I was next in line for the same treatment, which rather spoiled the piquancy of imagining Zarathustra in extremis.

'Ach, very well,' said I, curtly. 'What would I need to do, Moy?'

The froggy-faced fellow looked aghast. 'If you do not succeed, you will lose your mind.'

I shrugged. 'Something beastly is going to happen to me either way, it seems to me. I suggest I just get on with it, don't you?'

Moy frowned. He was listening hard. 'Wait! Quick! Hide!' And he ushered us out of the crystal cave, and into a dark recess in the passageway outside. We couldn't hear anything for a few moments, but it turned out that he was quite correct. A spider came trotting at full tilt towards us, heading towards the crystal chamber. He failed to notice us, thank goodness, as he crawled into the cave, presumably on some kind of routine work shift. That was what it looked like.

'Oh dear,' whispered Mrs Danby. 'Well, he's put paid to your rather dangerous-sounding idea, anyway.'

It rather seemed he had.

Except then Zarathustra did one of those things that, no matter how much he might at times infuriate me, will always win him a reprieve in my heart. He held out his hand to me. 'Could I borrow a handful of those wooden stakes you carry about, old fella?'

I handed them over without question. I could see that he meant business.

'Excuse me,' he told us. 'This is one of those occasions when brute force might be just the ticket.' Then he turned and hurried determinedly out of the shadows and back to the crystal cave.

'Oh dear,' fretted Mrs Danby. 'I do hope he...'

There came several sharp, strangulated squeals as Zarathustra plunged the stakes into the thorax of the newly-arrived spider. It died horribly in the confined space, thrashing its skinny legs about and almost beheading our Professor in the process.

'Oh glorious!' sang Moy the amphibian. 'How I have longed to see revenge upon these foul beings!'

Zarathustra emerged from the crystal cave, grinning happily and besmirched with gallons of purple spider's blood. Ach, horrible to see. But, I had to give him credit for being a dab hand with a stake. Perhaps I would let him accompany me on one of my missions one day, amongst the undead.

Mrs Danby and the others set to, dragging the spider's fresh corpse out of the cave. 'We must hurry,' Moy advised. 'This spider will soon be missed. They will realise that the sea creatures are no longer being controlled in this quadrant and then they will send others.'

I stepped up and prepared myself to take command of the crystal cave. 'Right then,' I said.

'Are you sure you can do it?' asked Martha. Fussing unnecessarily, I thought.

'I studied many kinds of mind tricks while I was in the Himalayas, Mrs Danby,' I told her. 'I am an expert on all sorts of astral planes. I am sure that I will soon get the hang of this.' I looked at Moy. 'Is there anything I must do? A special hat? Or wires or electrodes, perhaps?'

The amphibian gave me a strange look. 'No, none of that. Just use your mind. That's all we used to do, when we could do it. And it is all the spiders do. Just think. Channel your thoughts. And the miraculous crystals will do the rest.'

'I see,' said I, finding this whole thing absolutely fascinating, I must say. And also, just a tad alarming.

I took Martha Danby in my arms and kissed her gently on the forehead. She made a small noise in her throat.

'The Best of British, old chap,' said Zarathustra gruffly. As these adventures of his go on, he does tend to become more stiff-upper-lippish about the whole thing. It's quite remarkable.

Then I shook Moy's rather slippery hand and stepped into the crystal cave, alone.

I started to concentrate at once. I put all my thoughts into communicating with all the sea creatures within a five-mile radius.

'Denizens of the deep!' I thought. 'Monsters of the ocean! Kraken, awake! Serpents, cease your slumbers! Octopi – shake a leg! You must harken unto me. Doctor Van Halfling. Can you all hear my rallying cry? You toothsome sharks and barnacled whales? Electric eels and soaring manta rays. Listen to my commands! You must turn on these creatures who have colonized your peaceful world! You must seize your advantage and destroy the city of the spiders! Ach, be slaves no longer! Rip apart their protective domes! Let the ocean wash away your age-old oppressors! Come, do it now! Hear the voice of the one who commands you!'

Then, all of a sudden, I found I had said enough. I was suddenly exhausted. My own interior voice was ringing inside my head like a great, hellish klaxon. Ach, it was painful! But I had done my best. I had called out for help. For drastic measures. And now we must see what would come of it.

For a moment all was silent. The crystal walls all about me were glittering fiercely. But were they fiercer than before? Had any of this even worked?

First there were voices, from the passageway outside. I recognized the gasps and cries of my human companions. Then Moy's voice was crying out: 'Doctor Van Halfling! Look! Come and see! See what you have done!'

TWENTY-FIVE
MRS DANBY

My Dearest Nellie,

These were desperate times, indeed. Here we were – Zarathustra, Van Halfling and myself – and we were trapped at the bottom of the ocean, under the protective webbing of the city of the giant spiders. And now we were standing close to a crystal cave that was terribly important for some reason to do with mind control over all the creatures in the sea. I didn't quite follow the whole explanation – it did sound rather scientific and complicated for a humble housekeeper. Anyway, the upshot was, Abraham Van Halfling went into that crystal chamber and was using the powers of his mind to do something extraordinary.

The effects were plain to see, within minutes. I was standing by the viewing port, looking out at the dark seas immediately outside the city. There, an army of sea serpents, fanged and giant fish, frilled and deadly monsters of the deep were amassing. I saw octopi even bigger than the ones that had once troubled us. I saw colossal eels that lit up and shot sparks about the place. There were also things with vast mouths and needle-like teeth and eyes that stood out on stalks. They all looked absolutely furious at being summoned here, but they had no choice, as Moy explained. Abraham was calling upon the denizens of the deepest part of the ocean and exerting his will over them using a magic that had once belonged to Moy's own folk. These creatures had no choice but to obey.

And he was telling them to attack the city of Arachnopolis. He was goading them to rid the ocean floor of this unwanted scourge. Out there, the serpents and sea monsters were plainly bristling with long-harboured resentments. Their attack began almost at once.

'Magnificent beings!' Zarathustra was bellowing. 'Why, some of these have never been seen by human eyes!'

Just then, the whole tunnel we were in rocked and shuddered. Already we were feeling the impact of the assault.

'I could gladly have lived my life without ever having seen that lot,' I gasped. 'Horrible looking things!' It's true, I've never been fond of anything that came out of the sea, have I, Nellie? I never even liked cockles at the seaside.

But I was babbling, I realized, and so was Zarathustra, as he rhapsodized about the uncategorized species of fish that were about to bring us all to our doom. The city was reeling under the impact, and thin, spidery screams could be heard echoing from deep within Arachnopolis.

Then, the architect of our diversionary disaster, Abraham Van Halfling, was staggering out of the glowing cavern. Moy was supporting him as he went to observe what he had successfully wrought. Abraham didn't half look worse for wear. All that telepathic stuff had clearly taken it out of him.

He nodded in satisfaction as he saw what was happening. Even as the chamber we were in was buffeted and the lights flickered and dim, he looked pleased at the pandemonium. We watched a vast white whale emerge from the gloom and it seemed to be the size of a city itself. It stared at us with slow, rapacious greed through that tall window.

'They won't stop until the city is crushed,' Van Halfling said. 'But Moy, your people...?'

'We will be free to return to our ancient homes, in our own element,' the amphibian grinned. 'You have done us a great service.'

I couldn't help wondering how the spiders and their Queen would feel about what Van Halfling had done. As it turned out, I didn't have to wonder for long. No sooner had we left that viewing port and crystal chamber behind, heading back into the city proper, we soon became aware of the panicked, futile scattering of the spiders.

'They don't even know what's hit them,' Zarathustra said, with gruff satisfaction. It was so noisy now, he had to shout his loudest for us to hear.

'Them find! Them find!' screamed the Queen of Spiders. She quivered with panic. Her many eyes were out on stalks. Her fine black hair was standing on end on each of her rigid eight legs. 'Once at them find! This behind are they! It know I! It know I!'

She knew at once that somehow we had managed to bring destruction down on Arachnopolis. She could scent the foul ingenuity of human beings in this chaos and so she was screeching as soon as the first of the giant lampreys hit, crashing through the dome of webbing and letting the ocean pour in through the cracks. The Queen was screaming these words when we saw her, out on a wide plaza, under the fake night-time of the ocean's depths. She was with her retinue of courtiers, staring up at the sky. High above, whales were wheeling playfully like gigantic birds, smashing at the dome with their hefty tails. Sharks circled like vultures. The eels and manta rays wriggled excitedly as holes were dashed in the midnight skies and the oceans rained down, making all the spiders – including the Queen – scream aloud for mercy.

We saw it all. Zarathustra, Van Halfling, Moy and I. Moy was calling out to his fellow servants, as they flitted hither and thither, all of a panic. He told them their long-awaited revolution had come. The people from the surface were in the process of liberating Arachnopolis.

And so we were. All I could think, dear Nellie, was what a mess it was all going to make. Those golden towers and silk-spun bridges and walkways that the spiders had strung, so carefully, all were being smashed and washed away. There was death and disaster everywhere as spiders drowned and rubble rained down on us. But the water would wash it all away, and besides, cleaning up wasn't my responsibility here, thank goodness.

In fact, wouldn't we all be dead, as well? Weren't we all going to die together, in just a matter of minutes?

Zarathustra had lost his head. We were doomed, he said. These were our final few moments and we should meet them bravely, like English gentlemen. I took a glance upwards at the ocean about to pour down on us and informed him I was no such thing.

Van Halfling came struggling through the crush and push of the amphibious creatures that were currently milling excitedly around Moy (who was being treated something like a saviour!) and I was suddenly taken up in Abraham's wiry grasp. I actually found it rather reassuring to be held by him then. He said, 'Well, my dear. We have certainly known adventure and adversity before. Ach, but I see no way out for us this time.'

I had to agree. Yet I never felt in the slightest bit downcast, Nellie. You must believe me in this. I actually felt quite cheery.

'Wait!' shouted Professor Zarathustra. We looked at him and his eyes were alight with inspiration. His great black beard was bristling madly. 'The Magic Door! The Queen can control the Magic Door!'

We barely had time to absorb what he was saying before he raced past us, and was hurtling towards the chaotic plaza, where the Queen and her trusted courtiers were wailing and bemoaning their watery apocalypse. 'Your Majesty! Your Majesty!' Zarathustra cried, and all the spiders who hadn't yet drowned, were gazing at him in astonishment.

Abraham seized my arm rather harder than he needed to. 'What's the fool doing? He can't talk to them...!'

Moy put in, 'It looks as if he were bargaining with the Queen...'

That's precisely how it looked to me, too, as we took off at a stumbling run down towards that plaza. We knew we were taking our lives into our hands, by purposefully running towards that spidery elite, but we could not abandon Zarathustra, even if he had turned mad or traitorous, as I suspected.

'Door Magic?' screamed the Queen. 'Door Magic?'

Zarathustra was flapping his arms about, evidently trying to explain something to her. The other giant spiders were cringing in fear at the destruction going on around them, at the screams of the dying and the onrushing roar of the ocean. Van Halfling and I cautiously drew nearer, with Moy at our backs, just as the salty rain started to come down. We heard Zarathustra telling the Queen, 'Your Majesty, your means of escape is at hand. You colluded with Mumu: that much we know. You had access to the Threshold Technology, for that is how you intended to invade Earth. All I am suggesting now is that you bring forward your plans... and use it right now!'

I gasped in shock, and clutched the elderly vampire hunter by my side. Zarathustra was encouraging her to invade the world above? Simply in order to save his own skin? Yet we already knew he was prepared to go to enormous lengths to ensure his own survival.

'Drown will city my but!' howled the Queen, gesturing at the calamitous developments all around us. Even I could see that there was no stopping that destruction now. Arachnopolis was dead, and so were most of its spider inhabitants, and we had caused that.

'Come away, come away,' Zarathustra was coaxing her. 'Let us use the Magic Door...!'

And blow me – but she listened to him! She actually did what Zarathustra told her! She – along with her surviving spiders – and Zarathustra, and Moy, Van

Halfling and I – hurried back to the throne room that had once been so opulent and seemingly unassailable.

We found it several feet deep in icy cold water. A terrible shape surged out at us as we rounded a corner, and crunched noisily through the legs of several spiders. It was smooth, shiny and striped like a tiger, I noted, uselessly. I tried to jump backwards, and fell into the dingy, deadly spume. Van Halfling flashed forward with a stake in hand, but I grabbed him. There was no way I was about to let him waste time in trying to stake a shark. Instead I dragged him after the others, into the throne room, where the Queen was already up on her dais and scrambling towards her throne. She looked extremely panicked.

'You of all on revenge have will I!' came her high-pitched voice, as her fellow spiders crouched and moaned in the deepening water. It churned all around us, filthy with spider muck. Everything all at once seemed hopeless.

'Your Majesty,' prompted Professor Zarathustra loudly. 'Open the Magic Door!'

She raised two of her legs in the air and sketched the shape of a tall oblong in the air. 'Well very!' she said, and closed all of her eyes at once in concentration.

And the Magic Door appeared in the noisome air. Crimson and gold and humming with energy.

'W-will it take us away from here?' I asked Van Halfling. Our ears were full of the thunderous approach of the ocean, and we were soaked to the skin.

'We can only hope, my dear,' said Abraham, and held me to his side, where I was aware of the hard shape of his ever-present weaponry beneath his coat.

Without further ado, the Spider Queen flung open the door.

Beyond there was blackness. Nothing else. No indication at all where that threshold, once stepped over, would lead to.

'Your Majesty!' Zarathustra howled. 'Jump!'

She did, without further thought, cramming her whole bulky self through that doorway, even impossible though it may seem. A vast roar behind us caught my attention and I turned to see a tidal wave of death approaching at our backs. We all surged forward, robbed of all volition, apart from the desperate need to survive. Humans, amphibian, spiders and sea serpents: all of us flung ourselves at the Magic Door.

It gaped open to welcome us. Darkly, it glittered.

I remember hurtling towards it. My hand was held hard by Van Halfling. There were squealing arachnids breathing down our necks and the thrashing of their terrified limbs. There was the roar of the cold, massive ocean right on our heels...

And then we were falling.

Falling back down that peculiar, celestial spiral staircase that we had previously traversed on our way here to Arachnopolis. As the flashing lights plagued us once more and we tumbled and twirled into a dimension that only a chosen few have traversed, I hoped with all my heart that we would emerge where we had started.

I prayed desperately that we would be returned to the surface! I gritted my teeth and prayed like jiminy and still I held onto my vampire killer's hand.

Oh, please let us... please let us get home safe and sound!

To my Darling Wife, Mrs George Edward Zarathustra,

My dear, this is the ghastly climax to our adventure. This is the culmination of all of these bizarre events. In short, it's all about your magnificent husband Professor Zarathustra and how he fought giant spiders on the island of Manhattan!

For that was indeed where we suddenly were.

Oh, yes! The threshold technology, which had taken us to Arachnopolis – the city under the Atlantic – had brought us back again. Perhaps not as – ah – tidily, as we'd have liked. Things back in the throne room of the Queen Spider had become rather hectic.

In short, the doorway which brought us back home to the world above had appeared in the side of a building. The building where World of Mumu – the mystic travel agency had previously been. Something had gone awry, however, and the doorway had appeared some twenty feet up on the exterior wall, and our small party was propelled out into thin air.

What was worse – we were not alone.

At the time, of course we weren't sure what was going on at all. You try being flung through a Magic Door on the back of a tidal wave that is carrying you and several dozen giant spiders. And fish! All kinds of deep sea fish came pouring through the doorway with us, too. Big ones, small ones, peculiar ones. All of them doomed to die as they rained down on Lower Manhattan. The proprietors and chefs from dozens of nearby seafood restaurants came hurrying to our particular alleyway with buckets and basins. They could hardly believe their luck.

It was the day that it rained live fish, gigantic spiders and English Adventurers on New York.

All we knew about it at the time was being carried along in a huge, spuming, frothing rage of white water. We were aware of screaming and hurtling and then a lot of bright light. And then falling, very quickly, into the alley. And luckily one of the horrid giant spiders broke our fall, which didn't do him much good, but ensured our survival.

There we were: Doctor Van Halfling, Mrs Danby and myself, sitting on top of a dead spider, amongst the bins and squalor of a back alley. Staring up at a door-shaped hole in the wall above us, through which the whole Atlantic seemed to be pouring.

'We're back!' I cried, leaping to my feet, undaunted. 'Hurrah!' Then I spotted Moy, the Newt-man who had befriended and helped us in the city of the Spiders. He looked very shaky and surprised, supporting himself against a fence. 'Well done, Moy! You have helped save the day!'

Mrs Danby cut in sharply, 'But it was Abraham who did the hardest part. Using the crystal cave to telepathically command the sea serpents to attack the city and destroy it!'

I nodded and smiled, but I do think she was getting to be a bit too much in thrall to Van Halfling and his abilities. Certainly, he had mastered the telepathic crystal business. That was very impressive. Yet he had channelled all those powers into causing wanton destruction. Out in the Atlantic, way down on the ocean bed, the immensely beautiful structures that the spiders had taken more than a millennium to weave, would now be lying in rubble and tatters.

Now we could hear the sounds of sirens. Ambulances, police wagons and fire engines were all coming our way. What would they make of this apocalyptic scene when they saw it? Several spiders had landed in the alley. Soaked and crumpled, they looked rather smaller than we knew them to be. They crouched and cowered in the pouring rain and churning mess, but they didn't appear to be dead. The police were going to have a strange situation to deal with. Possibly a dangerous one. I started to look out for the Queen.

'I can't believe it, Abraham!' Mrs Danby was crying, sobbing and laughing at the same time. Over-reacting, of course. 'We're actually back in the human world!'

Already there were figures approaching down the alley from both ends. Sightseers come to see what was going on. They gasped and cowered at the thunderous roar of the waters as they continued to pour through that doorway.

'Shouldn't we think about finding a way to close the door again?' suggested Van Halfling. The noise was becoming even louder. It sounded like a dam breaking in the middle of the city.

'That would be a very good idea,' I agreed. 'But we don't know how, do we? The Queen might know, but I don't see her yet, amongst her wretched, half-drowned brethren. And Mumu the travel agent knew, but there's no sign of him, is there?'

'Then, if we can't shut it off,' shouted Mrs Danby, looking stricken. 'What will happen? Will the whole of the Atlantic ocean continue to come pouring through that little doorway? Will the whole city be drowned?'

Van Halfling frowned at her sharply, thinking her melodramatic. But she was quite right! We certainly weren't out of our predicament yet.

At this precise moment the Queen came through the doorway. She had gathered her legs in carefully, like a parachutist with his many ropes neatly tethered about him. She still somehow managed to look elegant and sinister as she came through the doorway. Some of the masonry and brick was starting to break away and crash down about our ears, enlarging the doorway and allowing her easier passage.

With a shriek of displeasure the Queen of the Spiders sprang through the air and landed in the alley amongst the rubble and the swirling saltwater.

There were horrified gasps from those who had never seen her before.

'This is hell fresh what?' she cried, with all her eyes staring up at the tall buildings around us.

We had no time to tell her anything. There came the cracking of gunfire from the mouth of the alley, and the whine of bullets as they struck bins and ricocheted off walls.

'They're firing on us!' screeched Mrs Danby, diving behind a heap of fallen rubble.

'Not at us,' snapped Van Halfling. 'At her!'

Yet the Spider Queen was impervious to the firepower of the New York Police Department. She shook herself dry and rose up – very impressively on her four back legs, turning to face her attackers. The bullets zinged off her glittering exoskeleton. Her hideous face was a mask of bitter disappointment and malice.

Still the ocean came pouring out of the wall. It was running away, crazily, out of both ends of the alleyway, carrying detritus and fish and fragments of the secret city of the spiders and the spiders themselves into the wider thoroughfares of Manhattan. From all around us there came the nasty, infuriating buzzing sound of chaos breaking out.

The police called in for more help. Those that weren't standing there, horrified, dumbstruck and terrified by the looming figure of the Giant Spider Queen. With an almost leisurely air, she reached out one leg and plucked up a young bobby. She regally inspected him and he was screaming as she gave him a little tasting, nibble nibble, with those caustic mandibles. Off came his head and his fellows howled in disgust and fear. They redoubled their firepower and the Queen of Spiderland just laughed at them. She said something about being warmly welcomed to her new environment, and how she intended to take over this entire world, sooner or later. All uttered backwards, of course, so no one but I really knew what she was saying, though her malevolent intent was plain enough. I think perhaps the Queen might have been starting to realise that invading the whole world might prove more arduous than she had imagined, back in the comfort of her throne room. It was taking her and her fellows long enough to get out of this alley.

But get out they did.

The giant spiders from under the sea re-gathered and regrouped and shook themselves dry. Under the command of their Queen they rallied themselves and prepared to attack the city. They emerged from that alleyway into the city streets of the East Village, striding leggily into the midst of the traffic, eliciting screams everywhere they went. Carriages careened into fire hydrants; horses reared up in atavistic panic. The spiders gazed up at those tall, steel and glass buildings and the gothic turrets of the older buildings and their black little hearts were thrilled at the sight. They launched themselves at this colossal new playground: scampering through impossible surfaces and vertical planes, peering in windows, stringing sticky new webwork between rooftops and towers.

'Look what we have unleashed upon New York City!' cried Doctor Van Halfling, as we tottered onto Broadway to see the carnage being wrought. Overturned cars were strewn in the middle of the street. Water was slewing across the road in great foaming gouts. It was hard to see where all this would end.

'This is a terrible sight,' Moy – our amphibian chum – stammered. 'We should never have used the Magic Door. Perhaps we will be responsible for the wanton destruction of two cities this day?'

I harrumphed and patted his back, making all the reassuring noises that I could. But I was starting to think he might be right. We had unleashed a horde of maddened and devilish spiders upon the second greatest city in the world! And they were free to do exactly as they pleased!

'We need help,' said I decisively. 'First things first.'

I turned and led my charges west, towards Washington Square and beyond.

'AH, MY DEAR ZARATHUSTRA! YOU BRAVE, BRAVE MAN!' CRIED HENRY GRENOBLE, the greatest mystic of his age. He greeted us on the doorstep of his Greenwich Village mansion and looked positively ecstatic to see us. 'And Mrs Danby! Doctor Van Halfling! And... and... a frog person.'

'This is Moy,' I introduced them. 'He was instrumental in helping us escape from the now-destroyed city of Arachnopolis. He's an amphibian person.'

What a dishevelled bunch we must have looked, wringing wet and exhausted on his doorstep. All of us were grimed with gluey muck from the spiders, and streaked with the slime and weed of the ocean depths. But we were alive!

We quickly briefed Henry Grenoble on the situation.

'Oh my,' he gabbled excitedly, stuffing his bag with odds and ends of magic potions and tricks and whirling on a sturdy Ulster coat. 'An army of giant spiders you say? Murder and mayhem on Broadway and the East Village?'

'They'll come this way, too,' said Mrs Danby urgently.

'The whole of New York will be swamped and subsumed,' added Van Halfling, taking great gloomy relish, as usual.

'Unless,' said I. 'A sorcerer possessed of terrific and awesome powers could find some way to close the Magic Door again.'

Henry Grenoble hoisted his bag over his shoulder and turned to kiss his worried-looking housekeeper, Rita, a brave goodbye. Then he led us back into the street saying, 'A doddle! A positive doddle, I'm sure!'

We hurried back to where we had come from, finding Washington Square in uproar. The tramps and students were fleeing in terror. Several of the spiders were sprawling all over the monuments and trees, exploring as they went. Henry Grenoble stopped to stare at them in delighted surprise. 'It's certainly true, Zarathustra,' he nodded approvingly. 'You still have a knack for summoning up monsters.'

'What about Mumu?' Mrs Danby said, struck by inspiration. 'Surely we can make him do something to help? It's all partly his fault, all this.'

Grenoble shook his head. 'I told you. When I appeared to you in my mystic form.'

'Oh yes,' she said. 'He'd vanished from the face of the earth. And the whole travel agency too.'

'As if it had never been,' said Henry Grenoble. 'But never mind that now! We have matters to attend to!'

So, with his worsted cloak swirling out behind him, he came with us to that certain alleyway, where the ocean was still pouring through.

In fact, things were worse. The doorway had been enlarged by the sheer force of the water. Now an aperture twenty feet wide was disgorging the Atlantic into our midst. With the greenish, bluish murk of the sea came all kinds of unaccountable forms, squirming and wriggling and gasping for breath.

We all stared in dismay at this peculiar spectacle. I rather wished I had my photographic equipment with me, my dear. There are fewer sights more bizarre than the one that confronted us that day. The police and bystanders had given up trying to stop it, or even comprehend it. They had fled the site, and were possibly being eaten or otherwise preoccupied by the oversized arachnids elsewhere.

Henry Grenoble was reaching around inside his carpet bag of mystic charms and chalices. He was humming and chanting and that third eye of his was out again, and glowing in a most alarming fashion.

'Ach, can you really do something about this ghastly situation?' asked Van

Halfling, tapping him on the shoulder. The imperturbability of Van Halfling is astonishing! The man hardly ever looks ruffled. Mrs Danby was white-faced with fear and I was bellowing, 'Do something! Nooooow, you three-eyed fool!!' for I had started to panic.

Henry Grenoble reached into his bag and pulled out a crystal ball, which was giving off purple fumes and making a truly terrible noise. He closed all of his eyes and gave his whole concentration to closing the Magic Door by using the evanescent powers of pure thought.

That's how he missed seeing the sea serpent coming through the hole.

We didn't, however.

We all stared at its fanged and horrid head as it thrust through what had once been the Magic Door. Yards and yards of silver serpent flesh came after it and we only had time to scream, together, at the tops of our voices as that horrible maw bore down upon us.

I remember a blast of fishy breath, hot as opening a pizza oven door.

And in that moment I knew we were doomed.

TWENTY-SEVEN
PROFESSOR
ZARATHUSTRA

To my Darling Wife, Mrs George Edward Zarathustra,

And now I approach the climax of my tale of our adventures in New York, my dear. You will hear that more tribulations were to come my way before this diabolical affair was finished with us!

As we stood underneath the 'door', watching the Atlantic Ocean spill on to the streets of Manhattan, we were arrested by the sight of a colossal and glittering sea serpent, slithering through the hole high up in the wall, gnashing and flashing its awful fangs at us. It was a terrifying beast.

At my side, the noted enchanter of Greenwich Village, Henry Grenoble, had his third eye out and all manner of mystical paraphernalia which he had brought with him. He was attempting to use his hexing powers to shut that doorway once and for all.

I must say that, at just that moment, it was looking pretty hopeless. Henry was muttering and his hands were lighting up and smoke was starting to come out of his crystal ball, but I wasn't holding out much hope. To encourage him, though, I slapped him hard upon the back: 'Come on, Henry, old fellow! Don't let us down now!'

And bugger me if the Magic Door didn't snap shut at once!

It went: thwaaapp! And that was that.

The deep sea beastie was sheared completely in half, as if by Madame Guillotine, and the front half dropped into the alleyway before it even knew it was dead. Those great silver jaws went on snapping and snarling at us even when it lay at our feet, writhing like billy-o.

Then we all turned to look at Henry Grenoble. Mrs Danby cried out, 'You did it! You actually did it, you wonderful man!' Then she proceeded to hug him in a most forceful manner. He gave a mere squeak in response, which sounded ever so loud now that the noise of rushing water had suddenly stopped. Then we were all cheering! All of our merry band! For we had saved Manhattan, hadn't we? We had saved the city from being deluged by the entire contents of the North Atlantic!

At this point I became aware that two men in sopping, bloody chef's aprons had appeared and were strenuously dragging the serpent's head and forequarters away. 'Hoi, the Natural History Museum will want that...!' But there was no telling them.

And besides, we had much more urgent business to attend to.

For the police came advancing on us, then. Clearly amazed and startled by the things that had been happening during this past hour, and looking wary of the half-serpent, to boot.

I girded my loins, as the first of the coppers arrived to plague us with questions. Who on Earth were we, and how were we mixed up in all of this?

The alleyway rang with questions and rebuttals and people all talking at once. I am afraid, my dear, that I did what you know I always do in such situations: I bellowed. 'Enough!'

'The giant spiders,' Mrs Danby reminded us earnestly. 'They are still running amok all over Manhattan!'

The venerable housekeeper was speaking the truth. And, as the most senior and responsible member of our team, I decided that we ought to present ourselves to the relevant authorities and pledge our help.

So that is how we came to be speaking with an army general and several rather severe-looking persons in uniform outside of City Hall, less than thirty minutes later. It seemed that a General Thomas was in charge of the hastily-organised operations.

He glared at us as if we were nothing but civilians. And, worse than that, senior citizens. As if we were doddering old fools capable of nothing but getting in the way.

'Sir!' I thundered at him, 'We can be of the most invaluable help. Yes, we do indeed know what a terrible situation you have here, with giant spiders causing untold disaster all over New York City. And we know because *we* brought them here!'

This made the general sit up and take note. He spat out his cigar and demanded to know what I meant by that.

I was in the process of explaining everything to do with the World of Mumu, Arachnopolis and the Queen of the Spiders and realized that the General was looking at me in a very strange way. 'Hey, you're that Professor Zarathustra guy!'

'I am indeed, sir,' I said, feeling glad to be recognized and given my dues. However, I loathe being referred to as a *guy* and so I gave him a very dark look.

'And these are your cronies!' the General said, looking at the others. Mrs Danby smiled prettily and Moy looked abashed.

'You must believe us,' Van Halfling said. 'We are inadvertently responsible for this calamity, and we'd like to help.'

The General still seemed rather sceptical at the sight of such a very dishevelled looking bunch. Gruffly he took us into his confidence and his hastily-organised operations room in City Hall, where he explained just how the armed forces and police were going about tackling the giant spider menace.

Our arachnid enemies had spread far and wide across the city in just an hour. Perhaps two hundred had spilled out of that trans-dimensional fissure in the warehouse. Now they were scurrying about in Battery Park, and as far north as Harlem. They had been reported swinging off the flashing lightshows of Times Square, and spinning themselves webby cradles between the tallest of the buildings on the Upper East Side. One hungry specimen had strolled across the Brooklyn Bridge, knocking cars aside and devouring pedestrians. One had even been spotted as far afield as Queens. From every corner of the island there came the ringing cries of panic, the wailing of sirens and the distinctive swishing of spiders spinning jumbo webs to ensnare new victims. Feebly struggling secretaries were suspended in cocoons from gables and gargoyles high atop the city.

'Oh my goodness,' gasped Mrs Danby. 'What have we done?'

'It was quite necessary,' I reassured her. 'It was the only way we could return home.'

Van Halfling was busily arguing with several men in uniform, who were intent on taking Moy into custody as an illegal alien. It took some time before they could be dissuaded, and by then I had had my brainwave.

'Bazookas!' I turned on the General and boomed at him. 'We need bazookas! That's all that will break through the chitinous skins of these beasts!'

Ordinary hand weapons were no good, of course. And it would take too long to get tanks up 5th, 6th and 7th Avenues, I was sure. But a number of bazookas dotted around the place, high up on buildings and carefully aimed. Surely they would be the best bet for ending this spider menace?

General Thomas looked dubious – and not as impressed by my idea as I expected. However, he went off to requisition the necessary equipment and it wasn't more than an hour later that we started to hear the not-too distant dull crumping noise of bazookas going off in the streets.

We went out into the city then, to see how operations were going. We saw the police force ushering along shocked-looking citizens. We saw soldiers dashing hither and thither. We moved northwards, up Broadway, through district after district, sometimes lost in the swirl of panicking people and subsiding waters. And all the while we could hear explosions going off and the defiant shrieks of the spiders at large.

'Ach, they are an intelligent species,' said Van Halfling glumly. 'A lost species. We should be making peace with them and learning from them...'

A particularly loud explosion shook the very ground under our feet. Really, I was terribly impressed by the American army's ability to amass weapons so quickly. And all at my instruction, too! That would never happen so efficiently at home. Just look at that do with the dinosaurs in Mayfair. However, Van Halfling had a point and I knew that, as a scientist of world renown I had a duty to try to protect both humans and spiders and to preserve life.

To that end I announced that I should like to communicate with the Queen of the spiders.

I learned from our friend General Thomas (who was rather revelling in the bloodshed, it must be said) that she was currently atop the tallest building in southern Manhattan, the Woolworth building. Her gigantic form could be seen for several blocks, etched against the smouldering skyline as she surveyed her new world. She was staring down at the explosions and the block fires and the mass exodus going on. And I thought it was high time that I had a word with her.

'Oh, my dear, brave Zarathustra,' wept Mrs Danby, when I announced my plan. 'You must be very careful.'

'Pah!' said I, for I care not for personal safety. Well, not much, anyhow.

So we went to Woolworths. Van Halfling, Moy and Mrs Danby all came with me. They wouldn't let me go alone. General Thomas and several others saw to it that no one got in our way as we took the lift to the very top of the elegant building.

And from there we had the same view as the Queen. This amazing vista of a futuristic city. Drenched in the waters from the deep, tainted with human and spider blood; in flames, in chaos.

She turned to face us from where she stood watching over her new domain. Those multiple, jewel-like eyes recognized us at once.

'If I offer myself to you,' I said, stepping bravely forward. 'Will you tell your people to cease the attack? Will the violence and destruction stop?'

She widened her eyes. 'Violence? Destruction? That started who?'

She claimed that all her spiders wanted was feeding. It had been we who had started slinging incendiaries around. That was true enough. But what are we supposed to do when nightmarish monsters invade our cities?

Again, I offered myself to her.

But her eyes fixed on Van Halfling. 'Yours than mind greater far a has he.' She was drooling as she said this, actually. It was quite repellent. As was Van Halfling's reaction. He became rather puffed up and noble.

'Him!' I gasped. 'Him? Rather than me?'

'Him,' insisted the Queen of the Spiders.

So there was nothing for it, I suddenly saw. I had to give way.

'Leave us,' Van Halfling told us all. 'Go back downstairs to Woolworths. I will give myself gladly for the sake of mankind.'

We all stared at him. I put my arm around Mrs Danby and turned to go.

'No!' she cried. 'I won't let you sacrifice yourself, Abraham!'

He turned to her sadly, and started unloading weapons from his voluminous coat. She held out her arms for his knives and stakes. 'I must, my dear,' he said.

'Good, good,' said the Queen. She was salivating more profusely now. Great long strings of spit were coming out of her mouth as she thought about sucking his brains out.

Mrs Danby wept as she hugged his arsenal to her bosom and then watched the man go to meet his fate.

The Spider Queen's twitchy, hairy legs reached out to meet him as he strode across the rooftop. She said something triumphant about how, with his knowledge, she would be able to take over all our world. I rather doubted it, somehow. I, Professor Zarathustra, knew that there would always be someone left to defeat multi-legged despots such as she.

'Van Halfling,' said the General, with all the army at his back. 'You don't have to do this. We can get a bazooka up in the lift. Just keep her talking and we can blow her to smithereens...'

But Van Halfling shook his head. He said to the Queen, 'You promise, don't you? To call off the attack? To tell your spiders to stop feeding and destroying? If I give myself willingly to you?'

'Yes, oh. Course of,' said the Queen. She grinned at him, horribly.

Mrs Danby buried her face in my shoulder. She couldn't bear to look any more.

And so she missed the final moment, when Van Halfling went walking into the Queen's embrace. He barely flinched as she took hold of him and started webbing him up at once. Fascinating to see, all that flossy stuff gushing out of her hindquarters and forming a perfect chrysalis about our elderly friend.

Then she tucked him under her thorax like a baby in a papoose and turned quickly, spinning herself off into the noise and smoke of the New York afternoon.

Mrs Danby broke down and I held her tightly.

Van Halfling was gone. But he had saved the city and perhaps the world. All by being extremely noble and impossibly brave and heroic.

Blast him!

My Dearest Nellie,

I imagine you will have read all about our goings-on in the newspapers and heard the most shocking details on the wireless. Yes, indeed, they had it substantially right and, for a few hours last Thursday, New York City was overrun by giant arachnids and almost flooded by the North Atlantic. And yet somehow – though this part hasn't been publicized – we were at the heart of it and saved the day. To the chagrin of Professor Zarathustra, our names are being kept out of it.

Principally, the name of that brave old chap, Abraham Van Halfling, is being kept out of the news. And yet it was he who sacrificed himself to our enemy the Queen. Once she had possession of him and his marvellous mind, she withdrew all of her forces and went underground. Literally, we are to believe. The spiders in the process of invading our world drew back and scattered into the deep recesses and tunnels that riddle Manhattan. It is said that those catacombs go as deep in some places as the skyscrapers have grown tall. Maybe there is enough world down there for the spiders? I hope they never emerge again. I hope that is the last we have seen of them. And I hope that Abraham is all right. I cannot believe that she will have killed such a wonderful man, simply in order to eat his brains. Or, with his great ingenuity, he has not found a way to escape from her foul clutches.

Except, my dear Nellie, that it is now a week later after our calamitous fracas with the spiders. The city has subsided into its usual splendid rackety chaos and it seems that everyone has forgotten the bizarre episode. Newer novelties have come to distract them since then.

But there has been no word of Doctor Van Halfling.

I myself had to speak with various people from colleges and universities across the USA. They phoned me at the Wellington, and telegraphed me there. I had to explain patiently to them that their guest lecturer would not be coming to see them. He would not, unfortunately, be able to honour their agreement and come to talk to them about his life fighting monsters and phantoms. For he has been taken away from us. Mostly they have been very understanding. Only one vice principal announced his intention to sue. One or two even asked if I would like to come and lecture to them about my life, instead! Imagine that, Nellie! Martha Danby! As if I've got anything to tell those learned gentlemen about.

So. Here I am in my room at the Wellington hotel on Seventh Avenue, at the end of my visit to New York. I am writing to you on fancy hotel stationery, and this letter will, I think, be the last one in this whole heap of pages I have spent much of the week writing to you. I want you to have the full, unexpurgated account of what has befallen me. Quite a rum tale it makes, too, I realise.

I wonder. I can't help mulling this over. It seems unfair when the old gent isn't even here, of course. But still I wonder. Would he have gone off, do you think? Abraham, I mean. If what happened hadn't happened, and if he had come through safely, like the rest of us. Would he have still gone off around the USA on his lecture tour? Or would he... perhaps... have called it all off? And stayed with me?

Oh, but I'm being silly, aren't I? He would have done his lectures and his duty, as a gentleman should. But when he returned to England, at long last, I wonder whether I should have seen him again? As more than just a friend or an acquaintance that he had once shared a terrifying adventure with?

But we will never know now, will we?

I folded up my new outfits and packed away the few things I have amassed on this trip in a new case I bought from a leather goods shop on Fifth Avenue. My bags are waiting by the door to be picked up by Billy, my friend who works here at the Wellington. I will have to leave the boy a decent tip. He listened to all my woes the other evening, over a nightcap in the lounge. I probably told him too much about recent events. He seemed quite surprised by it all.

Then, this morning, I had a visit.

I was in the foyer, having had my hair done in the salon downstairs. Then I heard a booming voice that I recognized in an instant. At first I shuddered and thought about ducking away. But I didn't. I turned and greeted Zarathustra with a smile and little peck on his cheek. I don't know, Nellie, but I think that bullish man might have been a bit chastened by our shocking adventures. He seems milder, somehow.

He had come to check up on me. He said that he didn't want me shooting off back to England before he could say goodbye. He seemed awkward and solicitous as he asked me to take a morning stroll with him. We were drawing attention from bystanders, some of whom obviously recognized the Professor from various interviews he had given during the week.

I went with him all the way downtown on the subway. As the train shuddered through tunnels I wondered about those darkest caverns under New York and the spiders skulking away down there. I didn't dare think too much about them, though. I wondered how long it would be before the army ventured down to find them, to try to do battle with them once more.

Professor Zarathustra noticed my worried expression. 'It's all over now, my dear,' he said, rather softly. 'Our ludicrous adventures are over at last. And I do apologise for dragging you into my world of mayhem and near-death.'

Or actual death, I thought sadly. Yet I couldn't quite let myself believe that Doctor Van Halfling could actually be dead. It just didn't seem like him.

We emerged from the subway at Christopher Street in the leafy and sunny environs of Greenwich Village. We went to Henry Grenoble's house for a light lunch, and to see how Moy, the amphibian boy, is settling in. He seems to be doing rather well. He has elected to become the Arch Mage's ward, and live in that rather elegant townhouse for the time being. Moy doesn't yet know how his own folk have got on, following the destruction of Arachnopolis, but Henry Grenoble has pledged to find out. The old enchanter is also hot on the trail of that weird travel agent, Mumu, though he tells us that the Chinaman seems to have slipped through the net and back to London, from whence he came in the first place.

It was good to see Moy, and to sit in Henry's conservatory, taking his strange tea and talking over our shared experiences. We even talked a little about Van Halfling, and I expressed my belief that he simply cannot be gone forever. I was aware of the men exchanging glances at this. I know they think me deluded.

Professor Zarathustra went on boastfully for a while, eating a whole plateful of dainty finger sandwiches, about how right he had been about the city of Arachnopolis, and how he had been vindicated in his knowledge that it truly existed.

'You were determined to find it,' I said. 'Come hell or high water.'

And then, for the first time, he explained why. He told us that it was because his wife has a terrible, incurable disease and less than a year to live. The rumours he had heard concerning an elixir of life to be found in the city at the bottom of the sea had been enough for him to pour all of his energies into discovering it. All for the sake of Mrs George Edward Zarathustra.

I must admit, this brought me up rather short. He was after a cure for his wife. It wasn't just selfishness and showing off. I think, my dear Nellie, that I have discovered hidden depths to Zarathustra. There has been more than just hubris and madness driving his actions. There has been love, as well.

Soon it was time to bid farewell to the magician of Greenwich Village and his new, amphibious, adopted son. I found myself promising to return to New York some day, to visit them. See that, Nellie? International travel is nothing to me now. See how I take it in my stride? Your sister has become a woman of the world, you see!

The housemaid, Rita brought our coats and we said goodbye, and Zarathustra and I strolled off through the Village in the sunshine. Already I was taking careful note of the time, and thinking about when I must be ready at my hotel with all my things together, and when the carriage would come to take me to the docks. I was sailing at midnight.

Funny, but I didn't feel at all nervous about travelling back across the Atlantic. Even after the sinking of the *SS Utopia* and almost dying several times. Surely the odds were against anything calamitous going on during my return trip? All I anticipated was a lazily luxurious cruise back to Southampton.

And then? What does my life hold in store for me, back in London?

Well, this is what I have to tell you, Nellie.

It all came out as I walked back uptown with Professor Zarathustra. We decided not to take the underground train again – preferring the sunlight to that noisy darkness. We wandered up Eighth Avenue and all of a sudden the Professor made me a proposition.

Not of *that* sort, Nellie! Of course not!

But it was – I admit – of a most intriguing kind.

He said, 'My dear Mrs Danby. I know that you have recently retired. You have hung up your housekeeper's pinny and cap. This time is your own. Your retirement. But I personally think that, having retired, you would shortly expire of utter boredom.'

'Do you?' I asked. Actually, I had been fretting over the very same thing.

He went on. 'I wonder... if you'd consider an offer I've been thinking of making you.'

'Go on,' I said. I was slightly wary. With Zarathustra you never really knew what was coming next.

We had walked as far as 42nd Street now, I saw. We turned east towards Broadway and eventually Times Square, the crowds growing thicker and noisier around us. I found myself looking forward to a bit of peace and quiet in England.

Professor Zarathustra said, 'You see, since my wife's illness made itself apparent and she has become as debilitated as she is, things have got rather messy and disorganized. Our house in Greenwich is not quite looking its best, I fear. We have servants, of course and a cook. But no one is whipping them into shape, I fear. My wife, quite naturally, is conserving her energy, and domestic tasks are the last thing I want her wasting her time on. And also, I need someone who can expend energy and time in whipping me into shape, Mrs Danby. I need someone who can keep me in check. A housekeeper, Mrs Danby!'

Under the glittering lights of Broadway – that valley of hopes and dreams and fantasies – I gasped at the very idea of being someone's housekeeper again. Getting used to their funny little ways. Being so involved in their lives. Learning a whole new way of life from scratch! In short, making a brand new beginning for myself!

He chuckled and scratched his enormous beard. 'I think, my dear, that if you were good enough for Mr Nightshade Jones, then you are good enough for Professor George Edward Zarathustra!'

I should think so too, I thought!

He walked alongside me, keen to get my reaction. Wanting me to agree. Hoping that I'd take the post. He was so impulsive, so ridiculous. His voice was booming out and people were looking.

Oh, am I mad for even considering it, Nellie? Or am I doing the right thing?

Well, I told him that I would think over his very kind offer and write to him from the ship during my return voyage. These matters were important, and could not be rushed. 'Of course, of course,' he said, looking absurdly hopeful as he delivered me to the awning at the front of my hotel. He made polite enquiries about my itinerary and time of sailing and so on. Then we said goodbye and I watched him hurry off across the road – not taking the crossing, as he should – and bellowing at cabs as they almost knocked him down.

Nellie, what if I took the post of housekeeper in London for him?

He is bound to drive me scatty. Or to get me embroiled in the midst of horrible danger, the likes of which I may never return from. Like poor old Abraham.

But on the other hand... I have found it all so very exciting, Nellie. Every minute of it. Even when we were under the ocean and seconds away from certain death. I feel rejuvenated by this small holiday of mine, even if nothing's gone as it was planned.

Anyhow. I will write to him from the sunbathing deck of the cruise ship – where I intend to spend much of the next week's sailing. And I will let him know my decision.

In the meantime I will finish up this long, long, long letter to you, my dearest sister Nellie. Bringing you up to date with the outrageous things that have been happening lately to me. And I'll package it up in brown paper and string and, before I quit this hotel, ask that nice boy Billy to post it for me. I know you like collecting the exotic stamps.

All my best wishes, dear, and I hope to see you in person before too long,

Love,

Your sister,

Martha

the End

DANBYI

ZARATHUSTRA!

VAN HALFLING!

ABOUT
THE AUTHOR

Paul Magrs lives and writes in Manchester. In a twenty year writing career he has published a number of novels in a variety of genres, including books about transtemporal adventuress Iris Wildthyme and also the Brenda and Effie Mysteries, which are about the Bride of Frankenstein running a B&B in the seaside town of Whitby. He has also written fiction for young adults, including *Strange Boy, Exchange* and most recently, *Lost on Mars* (Firefly Press.) Over the years he has contributed many times to the Doctor Who books and audio series. He is the author of a beloved cat memoir, *The Story of Fester Cat* (Berkley.) He has taught Creative Writing at both the University of East Anglia and Manchester Metropolitan University, and now writes full time.

His blog is at **www.lifeonmagrs.blogspot.co.uk** and he can be found on Twitter and Facebook.

Printed in Great Britain
by Amazon